DISCARD

CRAZY HORSE

CRAZY HORSE

JUDITH ST. GEORGE

G. P. PUTNAM'S SONS
NEW YORK

Library of Congress Cataloging-in-Publication Data
St. George, Judith. date
Crazy Horse / Judith St. George.   p.   cm.
Includes bibliographical references.
1. Crazy Horse. ca. 1842–1877—Juvenile literature.   2. Oglala
Indians—Biography—Juvenile literature.   3. Oglala Indians—Kings
and rulers—Juvenile literature.   4. Oglala Indians—Wars—Juvenile
literature.   [1. Crazy Horse, ca. 1842–1877.   2. Oglala Indians—
Biography.   3. Indians of North America—Biography.]   I. Title.
E99.O3C7294   1994   978'.004975'0092—dc20   [B]   94–12329 CIP AC
ISBN 0-399-22667-2

10   9   8   7   6   5   4   3   2   1

First impression

To Chance Alexander
with love

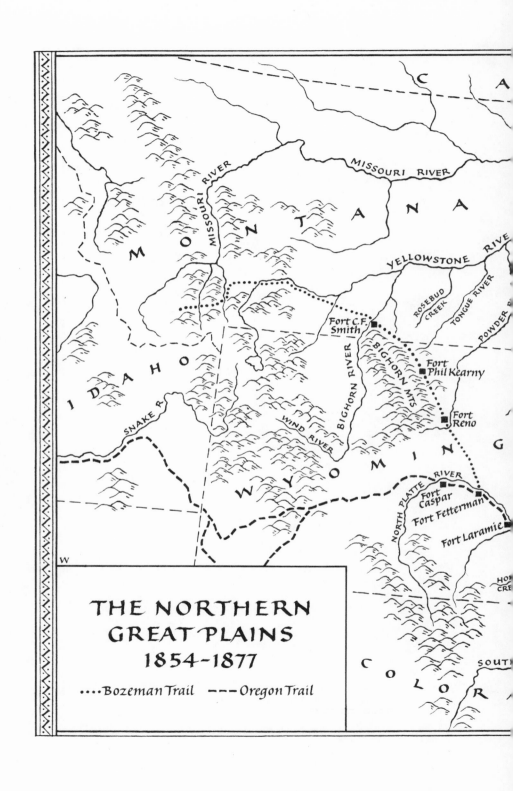

THE NORTHERN
GREAT PLAINS
1854–1877

···· Bozeman Trail   ––– Oregon Trail

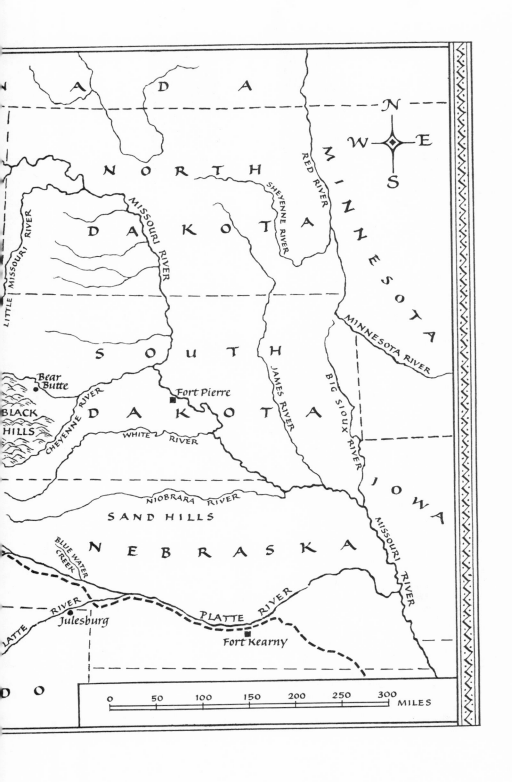

CRAZY HORSE

INTRODUCTION

My first encounter with Crazy Horse was some years ago when I traveled to South Dakota's Black Hills to research a book on Mount Rushmore. While in the Black Hills, my husband, David, and I visited the nearby Pine Ridge Sioux Reservation, the Sioux Indian Museum in Rapid City and the Korczak mountain sculpture of Crazy Horse and Indian Museum of North America. Our Black Hills stay opened a whole new vista to me, the appalling history of the Sioux Wars.

As time went on, that history nagged at me as a story to be told. And somehow, it was Crazy Horse who personified what the Plains people were fighting for—their freedom, their way of life, their land. But not much was known about Crazy Horse and I kept putting off the project until I learned of two primary sources, both available through the Nebraska State Historical Society. In 1930, Eleanor Hinman had interviewed men and women at the Pine Ridge and Rosebud Sioux Reservations who had known Crazy Horse personally. The

Ricker Tablets were transcripts of interviews with people who had lived through the Sioux Wars, newspaper articles, letters and some writings, which had been compiled by Nebraska's Judge E. S. Ricker.

As part of the research for the book, David and I returned to the Great Plains on what I called our Crazy Horse Journey. We drove 2,400 miles, traveling where Crazy Horse and his people had traveled, camped, hunted, wintered, fought and surrendered. Many people were wonderfully helpful on that journey: National and State Park superintendents and historians, Bureau of Land Management personnel, staffs of museums, historical societies, interpretative centers and visitor centers, as well as librarians and archivists.

On one memorable Big-Sky day, David and I headed out on a dirt road to find the marker where Fort Reno had once stood . . . and promptly got lost. For almost two hours we didn't see a person, house, car or even a fence or telephone pole. (We didn't find the marker, either.) As we drove through the rolling grasslands of Wyoming's Bighorn country, I became aware for the first time of how Crazy Horse and his people must have felt about the land, how they saw themselves as a part of nature and how every person, animal and plant had its place and purpose. Most of all, I was aware of how truly free they were.

But when it came to the book-research, I discovered that much of the source material was contradictory. Dates of events sometimes differed; Sioux and Army descriptions of battles often disagreed; the details of Crazy Horse's death varied from teller to teller. All I could do was weigh the evidence and make a judgment.

As with any biography, my response to Crazy Horse has been a personal one. Because he was a quiet, modest man who seldom spoke, there were times that I had to imagine what his emotions and reactions would have been, given his upbringing, character and mission in life. Although others might view him differently, I visualize him first and foremost as a man of, and for, his people . . . and only secondly as the celebrated Oglala warrior of Sioux Wars fame.

CHAPTER 1

Crazy Horse was thirteen in the Moon of the Ripe Plums, August, 1854, and not yet a warrior. Because of his light complexion and fine, light, wavy hair, he was known in his village as Curly. When Curly was eleven and had earned honors on a horse-catching expedition, his father, Crazy Horse, had given him the name Horse Stands in Sight. But the name didn't stick. So, until he had a life-changing dream, or did something significant that would give him his adult name, the boy was called Curly.

Curly was camped with his family and hundreds of other Sioux families close by the Holy Road, or what the whites called the Oregon Trail. For Curly, it was a happy time. There was great feasting and dancing and visiting back and forth between relatives and friends in other camps. And much like the past three summers, he and the other boys tended the pony herds, swam in the nearby North Platte River, raced their ponies and tested their skill against each other with bows and arrows.

Curly and his brother, Little Hawk, and his friends, Hump and Lone Bear, hung around the Holy Road, too, stopping the slow-moving covered wagons and pestering the whites for coffee and sugar and crackers. The older Sioux boys did more than just beg the white emigrants for treats. They raided the wagon trains, stealing an iron pot here, a rifle there, and even an occasional mule or cow that had wandered off.

As far as Curly and the others were concerned, no matter how much they begged or stole, it could never make up for how the endless stream of whites in their wagon trains had ruined these once-rich hunting grounds. With their guns and their wagon wheels, the whites had driven away the buffalo and the game. They had allowed their livestock to eat all the grass and they had cut down what little timber there was. And Curly hated the way the whites stared at his fair hair and light skin. Wondering if he were a white child who had been captured and raised by the Sioux, they pointed and used the word "captive." Although Curly didn't know what the word meant, their curiosity angered him.

Maybe one of the reasons that Curly and his friends' escapades on the Holy Road were so satisfying was that as much as the whites complained, they were too timid to do anything about it. As for the blue-coated soldiers stationed at nearby Fort Laramie, they weren't worth thinking about. There were only one hundred of them, certainly no threat to the thousands of Sioux camped only eight or nine miles to the east.

Actually, the soldiers stationed at Fort Laramie were as frustrated as the white emigrants whom they had been sent west to protect. There was hardly a wagon train that passed that wasn't heckled or plundered. These young Sioux acted as if they didn't even know that their chiefs had signed the

Horse Creek Treaty three years before that allowed wagon trains to travel safely on the Holy Road.

What was especially maddening to the soldiers was that for the past three years the Sioux had come to Fort Laramie to collect their $50,000 worth of food and supplies that the government had promised them in exchange for signing the treaty. It was time that the Army did something about the situation, and soon. Furthermore, any soldier could see that these Sioux were undisciplined and poorly armed, no match for combat-ready United States infantrymen.

The soldiers' opportunity would come sooner than they expected. It was almost dusk in the Sioux villages, the time of women cooking over their fires, when a number of Sioux boys (Curly might have been one of them) raced their ponies close by the Holy Road with a great whooping and hollering. Their high-pitched yelps startled a lame old cow being driven along by a Mormon farmer. Bolting, the cow plunged off the trail and headed for a circle of tipis beyond the road. Into the nearest tipi she charged, coming out the other side with a bundle on her horns. Panicked, she lumbered on, scattering kettles and tangling picket ropes as angry women pursued her, dogs barked and children ran to watch the excitement.

The farmer, who had chased his cow, stopped short at the edge of the Sioux encampment, alarmed at the sight of so many tipis. As he hesitated, deep within the circle came the crack of a gun. Everyone, including the farmer, knew what that meant. His cow had been shot. Perhaps afraid for his own life, the farmer fled back to his wagon, the sound of Sioux laughter following him.

It was no laughing matter to the farmer. Furious, he continued on his way to Fort Laramie where he demanded the arrest of the man who had killed his cow. After trying to talk the farmer out of such a drastic measure, the acting commander of the fort, Lieutenant Hugh Fleming, agreed to send for Conquering Bear, chief of all the Sioux, to parley the matter.

When the Horse Creek Treaty had been signed in 1851, the whites had appointed Conquering Bear to be head man of all the Sioux. Even Conquering Bear knew that the title was a paper one. "I would not have come here today if I had known this would happen," he had complained at the time. "I am not afraid to die, but to be chief of all the nation, I must be a big chief, or in a few moons I shall be dead on the prairie."

Those Sioux who lived on the Great Plains west of the Missouri River were made up of seven tribes: the Oglalas (Curly was an Oglala), Miniconjous, Brulés, Hunkpapas, Two Kettles, Blackfeet-Sioux and Sans Arcs. Because tribal leadership was always changing, no man ever served as permanent chief of any one tribe, let alone chief of all seven tribes. Although a man might be chosen chief of his village after leading a successful war party, he could just as easily be replaced for choosing a poor campground or failing to locate the buffalo herds.

Nevertheless, in an effort to keep the peace, Conquering Bear rode into Fort Laramie the following day to meet with Lieutenant Fleming. He first suggested that they wait until the new Indian Agent arrived so that he could settle the matter.

The answer was no. Fleming insisted that High Forehead, the Miniconjou brave who had killed the cow, be brought immediately to Fort Laramie for punishment.

Conquering Bear pointed out that the flesh of the old cow was so stringy that even cooked, it was hardly worth eating.

But Fleming wasn't interested in the condition of the cow. All he cared about was that High Forehead be brought in.

Conquering Bear next generously offered to let the farmer inspect his own fine pony herd and take whichever pony suited him in exchange for the wretched old cow.

The response was again no. High Forehead must be turned over to the Army.

Tempers began to rise. Fleming couldn't believe that Conquering Bear, chief of all the Sioux, wasn't able to control one hot-headed young warrior. Conquering Bear, on the other hand, resented this boyish blue-coated soldier telling him, Conquering Bear, an honored member of a Brulé warrior society, what he should or should not do. Still, Conquering Bear knew that the old men of the tribes wanted peace and he did his best. Well, then, he told Fleming, since High Forehead wasn't willing to surrender, it was up to the soldiers to come and get him.

Fleming agreed. They would ride out the next day. And with that simple remark, the war that would rage over the Great Plains for more than twenty years was set in motion.

CHAPTER 2

Conquering Bear left Fort Laramie and headed back to his Brulé village. On his way, he stopped at the Oglala village where Curly was camped with his father, Crazy Horse, his mother and his sister and brother. Calling together all the Oglala head men in their council lodge, Conquering Bear told them that the soldiers were marching out on the morrow to arrest High Forehead for killing the old cow.

Curly was as astonished as all the other Oglalas who were listening on the edge of the council lodge in the center of their tipi circle. (A lodge, which was larger than a tipi, was made of twenty-four buffalo skins to a tipi's eighteen.) Nothing like this had ever happened before. Once the soldiers marched a prisoner off in chains and irons, that prisoner was never seen again. To be bound in chains and irons had to be worse than death!

After Conquering Bear had left for his own village, anger buzzed around the Oglala camp like hornets disturbed in their nest. The old chiefs tried to calm everyone down. Their yearly gifts and rations were still in the warehouse, they said. Food supplies were almost gone and the children were growing hungry. They had to keep the peace until the new Indian Agent arrived and handed out their rations and annuities.

The young warriors wouldn't listen. Peace was all well and good for the old chiefs who had already won honors in war. But what about us? they demanded. We still have our war honors to win.

The next morning, Curly watched as the hot-blooded young warriors prepared for war. They stripped down to breechcloth and moccasins, painted their faces and bodies, tied their hair in knots over their foreheads, decorated their war ponies, knotted their ponies' tails and sang their brave-heart songs. More than one thousand Oglala and Brulé warriors, plus a handful of Miniconjous, were all girding for what was now, and always had been, central to their lives—warfare.

Warfare was central to Lieutenant John Grattan's life, too. Grattan, who had recently arrived at Fort Laramie from West Point, couldn't wait to take on the Sioux "savages" in a good fight. He had begged Lieutenant Fleming to allow him to lead a party of infantrymen into the Brulé camp to arrest High Forehead and permission had been granted.

Under an ominous red sky, Grattan and twenty-nine infantry volunteers, most of whom rode in wagons, along with a twelve-pound howitzer and a small mountain howitzer, headed out of Fort Laramie through the mud and muck of a recent rainstorm. Beside Grattan rode his interpreter, Lucien Auguste, whose father was a Frenchman and whose mother was an Iowa. The Sioux people hated Auguste. The man had little knowledge of their Lakota language and what was worse, he twisted their words into evil meanings. On this hot

11

nineteenth day of August, Lucien Auguste was already drunk.

As Grattan and his men made their way toward the Brulé encampment some eight miles from Fort Laramie, they passed a number of Sioux men standing around one of the trading posts where they traded their skins and robes for white man's goods. Auguste raced his horse up and down to give him a second wind the way the warriors did before a battle, waved his pistol and bellowed insults. Because the Sioux didn't have enough sense to listen to what they were told, he shouted, the soldiers would give them a new set of ears!

With trouble brewing, Curly itched to be in the thick of it. But he was too young to be a warrior and all he could do was ride up to the bluffs overlooking the Brulé encampment and watch. Although he couldn't hear what Auguste was shouting, he could follow the blue-coated soldiers and their gun wagons as they made their way past the Oglala village of his people and stopped at James Bordeaux's trading post. Again Auguste ran his horse up and down, and again brandished his pistol, yelling insults. The Sioux were all women. After he had them killed, he would eat their hearts out before sundown.

Although Conquering Bear and several other head men had ridden to Bordeaux's trading post to meet with Grattan, no amount of talk would change Grattan's mind. He was going to march his troops into the Brulé camp, find High Forehead and arrest him. But when Grattan and his men arrived at the Brulé village, the tipis were empty. The women and children had slipped away to take cover in the willows bordering the river and there were no men in sight.

Conquering Bear, who had also ridden back to the Brulé encampment, held another parley with Grattan. High Forehead refuses to surrender, Conquering Bear told Grattan, and in fact, he would rather die fighting than be taken prisoner. Conquering Bear repeated High Forehead's threat: "I have two guns and plenty of arrows and can fight."

Grattan would have none of it. Conquering Bear had no choice. He must turn over the Miniconjou. Seated on the ground, they parleyed back and forth as Curly continued to watch from above. Others were watching, too. Hundreds of Brulé and Oglala warriors were hidden in the nearby brush and willow thickets, ready and eager for battle.

But Man-Afraid-of-His-Horses, who was the respected head man of the Oglalas, was anxious to keep the peace. (His name meant that even his horses were feared.) Riding back to Bordeaux's trading post, he urged Bordeaux to come and interpret the parley in place of the drunken Auguste.

"My friend, come on," Man Afraid pleaded. "The interpreter is going to get us into a fight and they are going to fight if you don't come." Sensing trouble ahead, Bordeaux wouldn't budge.

Suddenly, after three-quarters of an hour of parleying, Grattan lost his patience, barked an order and jumped to one side. Curly heard the explosion of the howitzer and saw the tops of nearby tipis torn away. At the same time, gunshots rang out and Conquering Bear fell to the ground in a widening circle of blood.

With shrieks and war whoops, the Brulé and Oglala warriors galloped out of hiding. Grattan was killed instantly by a hail of arrows as the war party poured arrows, spears and tomahawks into the company of terrified soldiers. Some of the soldiers ran for the wagons but they, too, were killed. Although others took up a defensive position in a shallow depression, when they tried to escape, the mounted warriors charged, killing them all. In a matter of minutes, Grattan and his twenty-nine volunteers lay dead.

At the first shots, Auguste mounted his horse and fled back toward the Holy Road. He never made it. Blocking his path was a wall of Oglalas who first crippled his horse and then killed him. Although many warriors struck Auguste with their arrows and knives after he was dead, they didn't scalp him.

Curly waited until the fatally wounded Conquering Bear had been carried into his lodge and the warriors were gone before he and his friend, Lone Bear, rode their ponies down to where the soldiers' bodies lay. Loathing filled Curly's heart as he looked down at the body of Auguste, and in the ultimate Sioux insult, he lifted his breechcloth to stand naked above the staring eyes of the dead man. The time would come when he, too, would be a warrior. He would fight against the enemies of his people, achieve fame and honor in battle and above all, protect and provide for the old and helpless ones. It was his destiny and he knew it.

CHAPTER 3

The night after the battle, Curly and the other boys guarded the pony herds. After the noise and confusion of the day, the animals were skittish, and the warrior society, known as the *akicita,* wanted an eagle eye kept on the herds to make certain that none of the ponies stampeded.

Curly was skittish, too. Earlier, he had joined the young warriors in attacking the naked bodies of the soldiers, jumping them with their ponies, driving spears into them and burning the wagons and guns. Now these same warriors were newly painted, with fresh scalps hanging from their belts and bows. (Because the Sioux believed that the human spirit was somehow in, and of, human hair, an enemy scalp was a symbol of life, a sign of victory and a badge of honor, and not simply a bloodthirsty souvenir.)

Eager to avenge the shooting of Conquering Bear, the young warriors rode to James Bordeaux's trading post. From his station with the ponies, Curly could hear their war whoops and high thin war cries. If only he could see what was going on—but his duty was to guard the pony herds and that was what he would do.

Down at the trading post, the young warriors were demanding that James Bordeaux turn over the white emigrants who had taken refuge with him. But the fast-talking Bordeaux, with the help of the Brulé chief, Little Thunder, kept the warriors at bay throughout the night by giving out all his goods and wares.

Simply raiding Bordeaux's trading post wasn't enough for the young Sioux. In revenge for wounding Conquering Bear, they planned to ride to Fort Laramie at dawn, kill all the soldiers and burn down the fort. Little Thunder, the other tribal leaders and Bordeaux tried to talk them out of it. The whites might overlook what had happened to Grattan and his men and realize that it had all been caused by the soldiers' foolish shooting of Conquering Bear, they pointed out. But if more whites were killed and the fort burned, the Great White Father, the President, was sure to send many wagonfuls of soldiers against them.

In the end, it was the women who settled the argument. Anxious for the children and old ones to be far from the trouble, they packed up their tipis and began to move out across the North Platte River. The warriors had no choice. Because their first responsibility was to protect the women, the young and the helpless ones, they, too, moved out. Before they left, however, they made a quick raid on the other traders' buildings and captured Bordeaux's herd of cattle and most of his horses.

After crossing the North Platte River, the Oglalas and the Brulés separated. The Oglalas headed north for a buffalo hunt, while the Brulés, led by Little Thunder and Spotted Tail, rode northeast into the Sand Hills. Although Curly's father was an Oglala, his mother was the Brulé sister of Spotted Tail, and in times of trouble, Sioux families went with the wife's tribe. And so, Curly, his parents, sister and brother traveled with the Brulés.

Like everyone else, Curly enjoyed being on the move. He and his friends would ride their ponies across the open prairie in endless races, while the women gossiped back and forth and the older boys sang and showed off for the girls. But with six of the strongest Brulé warriors carrying the wounded Conquering Bear in a buffalo hide sling, the Brulés moved as quickly and quietly as they could.

Days later, they reached their destination, their old hunting grounds on the Running Water River (now Niobrara River), where they set up camp. The rolling, treeless Sand Hills were wonderfully rich in game—elk, deer, antelope, fox, raccoon, badger, porcupine, beaver and muskrat, as well as ducks, geese, quail, curlew, snow birds, prairie chickens, pigeons, cranes and grouse. And nothing tasted better than the sweet roasted meat of the rabbits that Curly and the other boys snared by the droves. The Sand Hills were rich, too, in prairie turnips, wild onions, gooseberries, chokecherries, juneberries, plums, roseberries, acorns and cactus fruit.

Despite the Brulés' pleasure at being in their old hunting grounds, a sadness hung over the camp. Conquering Bear was dying. Only the men needed to lift him in and out of his sling, the medicine man and the holy man, who listened and gave advice, were allowed in his lodge. Although the *akicita* society stood guard, one morning Curly happened to be passing by when the lodge door flap opened and he saw inside. He was shocked at the sight of the dying man. Conquering Bear's yellow skin was stretched taut over his cheekbones and his eyes were dark circles in his skull-like face. And from the lodge came the unmistakable smell of death.

Deeply moved, Curly felt the need to be alone to ponder on what had happened, how Conquering Bear, despite his effort to keep the peace, now lay dying from the soldiers' guns. He mounted his pinto pony and rode hard away from camp. Although several of his friends tried to join him, he angrily turned them back.

Curly was different and his friends respected that. He was not only shorter and slighter than the other boys his age, but he was also shy and modest. Often withdrawn, he was seldom loud and boisterous like his friends. Even though he excelled in the pony races, shot his arrows as fast and far as anyone else and never flinched in the rough-and-tumble games they played, he didn't brag or sing of his triumphs as the others did.

This day, Curly had a special reason for wanting to be alone. Now that he was thirteen, he had decided that it was time to seek his vision, a vision that would direct the future course of his life. He rode a good distance from camp to a high bluff overlooking a lake and hobbled his pony close to grass and water. Stripping down to his breechcloth and moccasins, he stretched out on a gravel bed and prepared to go without food, water and sleep for however long it took for his vision, or dream, to come to him.

From what other young men had said about their own experiences, he was certain that an animal would speak to him, and although he might not understand the message, a holy man would later interpret the animal's words. Curly also knew that no matter how his vision directed him, whether toward becoming a warrior, hunter, scout, horse-catcher, historian, medicine man, holy man like his father, even a

18

heyoka, or clown, that life-course would be honored by every member of his tribe.

But no vision came to Curly. Desperate to keep himself awake, he piled sharp stones under his bare back and between his toes. He tried to sing as others had told of singing, but no song came to him. For two days and two nights, he lay there, hot with the scorching sun of the day and shivering through the star-studded prairie nights. His tongue was swollen from lack of water and his eyes burned from lack of sleep. Perhaps he wasn't worthy. He knew that he wasn't like the other boys. His hair and complexion were light and he had always been smaller and slighter, too. Then there was his dislike of painting himself or wearing beads, and he had no taste for dancing or singing or boasting, although it was expected of him.

Discouraged by his failure, Curly rose on the third day and stumbled back to where he had hobbled his pony by the lake. Weak from fasting, he tripped and fell and it was then that a dream came to him. A man dressed in a plain shirt and buckskin leggings came riding up out of the lake on horseback. He was wearing only one feather in his long, flowing brown hair and he had a small stone tied behind his ear.

The man, whose face was unpainted, told Curly that he was never to wear a war bonnet or tie up his pony's tail for war. Before going into battle, Curly should pass dust over his pony in lines and streaks but should never paint him. Curly was also to pass dirt over his own hair and body. If he did, he would never be killed by a bullet or by the enemy. After a battle was over, Curly must remember not to take anything for himself.

As the man spoke, he was riding through flying arrows and bullets which disappeared before they struck him. Although

19

the man's own people appeared behind him several times and pinned back his arms, he was able to shake them off and ride on. A storm came up and a zigzag of lightning appeared on the man's cheek, as well as hail spots on his body, which was now clothed only in a breechcloth. As the storm passed, the man's people again closed in around him, grabbing and pulling at him while overhead a hawk screeched. At that moment, the dream faded and Curly awoke.

It wasn't much of a vision as far as Curly was concerned. Why, no animal had even spoken to him! Perhaps if he stayed on, he would have a more significant dream. Exhausted, Curly fell asleep. This time when he awoke, his father, Crazy Horse, and his *kola,* his best friend, Hump, were standing over him. And his father was very angry. No one knew where Curly had gone, he scolded. Crow or Pawnee raiding parties might be nearby. He could have been captured or killed.

Curly tried to explain. He had come out here by himself to seek his vision.

His father became even angrier. His vision! How dare Curly take that important step upon himself without making preparations? He hadn't consulted with the wise ones or been purified in a sweat lodge.

Distressed that he had been the cause of so much concern, Curly mounted his pony and silently followed his father and Hump back to camp without mentioning his dream. And he didn't have the opportunity to tell his father about his dream in the days to come. Conquering Bear died and the Brulés went into mourning.

Relatives dressed Conquering Bear's body in his finest clothes and placed his weapons, war paint and eagle-bone flute beside him. They wrapped his body and belongings first in a robe, and then in a tanned buffalo skin. Family members

20

gashed their arms and legs, loosened and cut their hair and covered themselves with dust as they wept and wailed their songs of grief.

After four days of mourning, Conquering Bear's body was carried from his lodge and laid on a high platform called a death scaffold. His favorite pony, painted with red blotches and covered with a robe, was shot and his tail hung from a scaffold post. Conquering Bear's shield, medicine pouch, drum and lance were hung on another post so that he would have all his familiar possessions with him in the next life, the Land of Many Lodges.

When the ceremonies were over, the people returned to their village, sober and saddened. Conquering Bear had been a peace-chief, and as his reward, the soldiers had killed him. Now those soldiers were all dead, too. Young as he was, perhaps Curly realized, as his people must have, that there would be no going back to how life had been before. A new path lay ahead.

CHAPTER 4

Wide Vs of geese flew overhead, their honking mixed with the call of thousands of ducks, cranes, herons and other waterbirds, all headed south. In the distant hills, the bull elk bugled his mating song, while the Sand Hill grasses were in their fall colors of pink, purple, orange and yellow. Winter was coming and everyone in the Brulé camp was concerned about food for the coming months, especially the women.

For twenty years, the Sioux had traded hides and skins with the white traders down by Fort Laramie for foodstuffs and goods—coffee, tobacco, sugar, molasses, raisins, crackers, beans, bacon, blankets, kettles, calico, glass beads, even iron for their arrow and spear points. And whiskey, too. Curly had seen what whiskey did to his people. They were unaccustomed to liquor, and their drinking had led to accidents, family quarrels, fights, even murder.

Although the whiskey caused nothing but trouble, the people had become dependent on the trader goods, and now they would be without them through the long, hard Plains winter. The soldiers were angry. There would be no returning to the traders' stores along the Holy Road, nor would the traders be allowed to bring their packs and wagons into the Sioux camps during the winter months the way they always had.

With no buffalo meat drying on the racks, the women's large buffalo-skin boxes called parfleches, which held dried food for winter eating, were empty. Although it was time for the people to be on the move for their fall buffalo hunt, the buffalo, or bison, their source of life, was hiding from them.

It was Curly who found them. On a deer-hunting expedition, several days' distance from camp, Curly sensed, rather than heard, the presence of a buffalo herd. Maybe in his eagerness to find buffalo, his imagination was playing tricks on him. To make sure, he got down on all fours and pressed his ear to the ground. From far off, two, maybe three, days' travel away, he felt the earth rumble under the running weight of many thousands of buffalo.

As the Brulé head man, Iron Shell, said: "Such things as cherries and even buffalo don't stay around long and the people must get them when they can." Curly pushed his pinto hard to return to camp as fast as he could. Galloping in, he called out his good news.

The people were as excited as Curly was. That night, Curly's father, Crazy Horse, gave special thanks by taking his long-stemmed, sacred stone pipe from its stand and going to a high place. Alone, he lit his pipe and offered the stem to the Spirit Above, the Mother Earth and to the four directions, or four winds, east, south, west and north. Singing a song of a hungry people who needed the buffalo for the winter, Crazy Horse sang a song for his son, too, to make him strong, this

23

strange, modest, light-haired boy of his, unlike the others. When Crazy Horse finished singing, he sat smoking his pipe until a sliver of a moon began to rise over the hills.

The next morning brought the great moving of the camp. "Now take it down, down!" the village crier ordered. "Many bison I have heard; many bison I have heard!" Immediately, the women struck their tipis, packed up their belongings into bundles and hung them on their saddles, along with their babies strapped in cradleboards. They then lashed the tipi poles to their ponies to make a frame called a pony drag, or travois, that would drag behind the pony to hold more bundles. Willow cages were tied to some of the travois in which the old and helpless ones rode, as well as children who were too big for a cradleboard but not yet able to ride on their own.

In honor of the occasion, the women, who were adorned with handsome rings, bracelets and armlets, wore their finest doeskin dresses decorated with elk teeth. They rode their best ponies, their saddle trappings decorated with beautiful bead- and quillwork.

Led by the four old-man chiefs carrying the fire of the village, Curly and his family traveled with the Brulés for three days before the scouts who had been sent on ahead returned. Riding into the council lodge in the center of the tipi circle, the scouts reported that they had found the buffalo herd that Curly had heard, enough buffalo to make even the hungriest Brulé happy. And the buffalo, heavy with fat for the winter ahead, had already grown their winter coats that would make warm robes, winter tipi linings and floor coverings.

After the scouts told the head men where they had seen the buffalo, the crier again paraded around the tipi circle with his message:

24

Your knives shall be sharpened,
   your arrows shall be sharpened.
Make ready, make haste; your horses make ready!
We shall go forth with arrows.
   Plenty of meat we shall make!

Quickly the women packed, and before the sun was fully up, the camp was on the move again. The *akicita* led the way, riding twenty abreast, with their ponies shoulder-to-shoulder so that no one could break rank. Eager for glory, the young men had been known to gallop on ahead to kill the first buffalo, or the largest, or the greatest number, and by doing so, had stampeded the whole herd. Behind the *akicita*, the hunters rode five abreast, each leading his trained buffalo pony. Last came the people, protected on all sides by the warriors, as always.

While still on the move, the head men selected the best hunters with the fastest ponies for a special honor. Any buffalo these hunters killed would be given to the members of the village who had no one to provide for them. (Curly was too young for such an honor.) "Today you shall feed the helpless," they were told. "Perhaps there are some old and feeble people without sons, or some who have little children and no man. You shall help these, and whatever you kill shall be theirs."

As soon as the buffalo herd was sighted, everyone knew that Curly had spoken true. The prairie was brown from horizon to horizon with the feeding animals, the sound of their snuffling and grunting like a gift from Wakan Tanka, the Great Spirit.

Stripped down to their breechcloths and moccasins, Curly and the other hunters mounted their buffalo ponies bareback, using only a jaw rope to guide them. With quivers of arrows over their left shoulders, they grasped their bows in one hand and their quirts, or whips, in the other. Always downwind of the buffalo, which counted on their sense of smell to warn them of danger, the hunters divided into two groups. As soon as they had encircled the feeding herd on either side in a surround, the order came: "Hoka hey! Charge!"

At the shout, the buffalo stopped and sniffed. Their tails went up and they started to run, their pounding hoofs kicking up a tower of dust. But the buffalo were trapped. The hunters rode in sideways, past the old bulls which guarded the herd to get at the fat cows and young calves in the center.

Danger was everywhere. Wounded buffalo pawed the ground and charged. Ponies stumbled and fell. Other ponies were gored by the enraged beasts and their riders thrown under the sharp hoofs of the stampeding herd. But the hunters had been trained all their lives to confront danger and no one hesitated. Each time a hunter killed a buffalo, he cried out, "Yihoo!" Soon the air was filled with the dust of thundering hoofs, the smell of blood, the bawling of wounded buffalo and the shouts of triumph.

"Yihoo!" Curly yelled as he aimed his arrow into the left shoulder of a yearling to reach the heart. Although he killed the yearling easily, a two-year-old was harder to fell. When his first arrow hit, the animal went down, but only briefly. Quick! Another arrow! And another! And another! Curly had to shoot four arrows with all his strength before the buffalo dropped with a dying bellow.

When all their arrows had been spent, and the prairie was blanketed with the bodies of the buffalo, the hunters searched out their own specially marked arrows to claim their kill. As they began to butcher the meat, the women ran down from

26

the nearby hilltop where they had been watching, their voices all raised in a trilling song of joy. With long knives, they peeled back the skins from the fat meat, while the children darted in and out, begging for tidbits of raw liver. It was sunset before they finished the butchering and loaded the great slabs of red meat on the pack ponies, along with hide sacks filled with skins.

Back at camp, Curly's mother and the other women cut the meat into thin, flat strips and hung them on the drying racks as the smell of roasted meat blended with the blue smoke from the cooking fires. Later, the women would pound the dried meat and mix it with animal fat and dried berries to make pemmican for winter eating.

But the buffalo provided more than just food. At the heart of Sioux life, the buffalo provided clothing, robes, weapons, tools, fuel, tipis, utensils, thread, paintbrushes, soap, glue, water buckets and more. It was little wonder that the people selected the finest buffalo skin from the hunt for a special offering. When they had painted and trimmed it with dyed porcupine quills and beads, they spread it out on a hilltop as a thanksgiving gift to their brother, the buffalo.

That night the drums beat as the people danced and sang their joy and gratitude. And then a hunter stood up and walked around the fire singing of one who was still young, who had never sat on the council, who was not a member of the *akicita*. But he had been given a great gift, the gift of ears.

All eyes turned toward Curly, for everyone knew that it was Curly who had first heard the buffalo. But as the hunter continued to circle the fire and sing his song of praise, Curly pulled back into the shadows. He didn't want to be singled out for honors. It was honor enough that his people would have food, shelter and warm clothing for the winter ahead.

27

CHAPTER 5

With the buffalo hides cured, and a good supply of buffalo meat stored away for the winter, Conquering Bear's family prepared to avenge his death. In the Moon of the Hairless Calves, November, 1854, Conquering Bear's two brothers, Red Leaf and Long Chin, and his nephew, Spotted Tail, dressed for war, sang their war songs and headed for the Holy Road to attack any whites whom they could find. (Throughout the Sioux Wars, whites killed innocent Sioux and Cheyennes in revenge for white deaths, while Sioux and Cheyennes killed innocent whites in revenge for Sioux and Cheyenne deaths.)

It was late in the year and there were few travelers on the Holy Road. Taking cover in the brush near the site where the Horse Creek Treaty had been signed three years before, some thirty-seven miles east of Fort Laramie, the Brulé warriors sighted a swirl of dust in the distance. A team of mules drawing a box wagon that the whites called a mail coach was approaching. As the wagon drew alongside their hiding place, the warriors opened fire, killing the two men sitting on the driver's seat and a passenger riding inside.

Swooping down on the wagon, the three Brulés pulled out an iron box filled with gold coins and sheaves of paper. Knowing that the gold coins were valuable, they divided the money among themselves to buy goods at the traders' stores. As for the pieces of paper, they filled them with tobacco and willow bark to make cigarettes the way they had seen the whites do. What paper scraps were left over, they flung to the November winds, laughing as they fluttered and blew away. But when they told James Bordeaux, the trader, how they had torn up the paper, he paled. That was paper money and as valuable as the gold coins, he explained. It was worth many thousands of dollars.

By now, Curly and his family had left the Brulés and returned to spend the winter in the Oglala camp of Curly's father, well north of Fort Laramie and the Holy Road. As always, the winter camp where they would spend the next four or five months was comfortably located beside a sheltered stream. The cottonwood trees that grew along the water's banks provided wood for fuel and bark for the ponies to eat when there was no longer grass under the snow.

Delighted to be reunited with his friends, Curly spent most of that fall and winter on hunting expeditions with Hump and Lone Bear. Despite the cold and snow, game was so plentiful that those Sioux who were camped all year around near Fort Laramie, living on handouts, traveled north to share in the good eating and good talk around the Oglala campfires.

Called Loaf-Around-the-Forts, or Loafers, the Sioux visitors gleefully recounted how the three Brulé warriors had attacked the mail coach. The best part of it was that the soldiers hadn't made a move to arrest them, not even when the warriors had visited the traders' houses afterwards telling everyone what they had done. Furthermore, the Loafers reported, not only were the soldiers at Fort Laramie weak and few in number, but because of what had happened to Grattan and his troops after the cow-trouble, they were also very much afraid. Come spring, though, it would be different. There was talk of a large force of soldiers arriving at the fort.

Curly listened, but as usual, said little. He knew that when the snows were gone, the Holy Road would once again be crowded with wagons headed west carrying guns and ammunition and good things to eat. And since the soldiers were so fearful, mules, cattle and big American horses might make for easy pickings, too. After all, the whites had ruined the whole North Platte valley with their wagon trains and they should be made to pay for what they had done.

Although the Oglalas stayed north, far from any trouble, Curly left his family after the annual Sun Dance and headed south in the Moon of the Ripe Juneberries, June. There, he rejoined his uncle Spotted Tail and his other Brulé relatives at Chief Little Thunder's camp south of the Holy Road.

Like most Sioux boys, Curly had sneaked off on his first horse-stealing party when he was about eleven and, although the warriors had carefully kept him out of danger, the experience had been heady. Now that he was fourteen, in the Moon of the Ripening Chokecherries, July, 1855, Chief Little Thunder and his second in command, Spotted Tail, included him in a horse-stealing expedition. (Actually, the Sioux' small sturdy mounts were ponies rather than horses.)

Stealing horses from the enemy, which usually involved a good fight as well, was what a Sioux warrior's life was all about. Not only were horses essential for warfare, hunting and travel, but they were also used as a gift to a family to win

30

a daughter in marriage, a treasured trophy from a successful raid, an apology offered for an insult, a thank-you for a favor, a donation to the helpless ones.

Because the horse-stealing expedition numbered many men, it soon split in two. Little Thunder and his Brulés headed south to the Pawnee camping grounds, while Curly rode east under Spotted Tail to Omaha country, farther east than he had ever been before.

After days of travel, Curly's party came upon the night camp of a band of Omahas. At the first glimmer of dawn, the Brulés noiselessly crept up on the pony herds, cut the hobbles on the finest ponies and took off with them. When the enraged Omahas discovered the theft, they headed out in pursuit, just as the Brulés had anticipated they would. As soon as the Omaha warriors disappeared, the Brulés circled back to attack the unprotected Omaha camp. When the Omahas realized that they had been tricked, they returned to their camp at a gallop to protect their women and children and to recapture their ponies.

During the hard three-hour battle that followed, Curly caught sight of an Omaha sneaking off into the brush. He drew his bow taut and shot his arrow straight. The Omaha jerked back, and then slumped forward. It was Curly's first kill. Pulling out his scalping knife, he ran toward the brush. But when he took hold of the Omaha's hair, he was startled to see that he had killed a woman. There was no disgrace in that. Since a warrior would always fight harder to protect a woman during a battle than he would another man, or even himself, killing an enemy woman brought honor. This woman, though, was young and pretty, with shiny long braids like his sister's, and Curly couldn't bring himself to scalp her. Turning away, he left the scalping to others.

Well pleased with their success, the Brulés were in a

31

triumphant mood as they rode back to their camp. They had captured fine ponies, taken four Omaha scalps, including the chief's, and counted many coups. Counting coup in battle was riding or approaching an enemy, either mounted or on foot, and touching that enemy with a hand, a coup stick or a weapon. Because it was impossible to shoot an arrow or use a weapon at the same time, counting coup on an enemy took more courage and earned a warrior as much, if not more, prestige than killing him. Coup could also be counted on a fallen enemy, a victory in hand-to-hand fighting, saving a friend in battle, stealing a horse, or any other brave deed.

Yet here was Curly, already known for his daring, who wouldn't even take a woman's scalp. To pass the time on their long journey home, the Brulés teased Curly with a song.

> *A brave young man comes here*
> *But a foolish one,*
> *Without a good knife.*

The Sioux loved to tease (and hated to be teased) and although the song may have stung, Curly joined in the laughter. Nevertheless, he offered no explanation. It was only later, as an adult, that he admitted that he had never been happy with the way that his people treated enemy women.

Curly, who had only one sister, had lost his mother when he was very young. (The woman whom he called Mother was his mother's sister, his father's second wife.) Curly didn't know much about women except that it was the women of his tipi and village who provided care and warmth and love. Some day he, too, would be married and have a tipi of his own where he would know the warmth and love of his own woman.

CHAPTER 6

Throughout the summer of 1855, Curly raided the Holy Road with his Brulé friends. They stole a mule here, a cow there, badgered the emigrants for treats or even surrounded their wagons demanding guns and ammunition, or just sugar and coffee, in exchange for safe passage.

Staging hit-and-run raids, with no overall plan or united teamwork, was how the Sioux had always waged war against their tribal enemies. That same kind of harassment, they were sure, would be enough to discourage the whites from using the Holy Road. And they had proof. No one, including the soldiers at Fort Laramie, did anything to stop them. Soon the flood of wagon trains would end, the grass would grow tall again, the buffalo and game would return and once again this North Platte valley would be prime hunting grounds.

But just as the Fort Laramie Loafers had predicted, the soldiers had plans, big plans. In the Moon of the Ripe Plums, August, the new Indian Agent at Fort Laramie sent out runners to all the Sioux camps ordering them to "come in." If they came into Fort Laramie, the Army would protect them. If they stayed out, they would be considered hostiles and be dealt with as enemies of the United States government. Within a few weeks, more than half the Sioux bands, including most of the Oglalas, had come in. They set up their four hundred lodges not far from Fort Laramie, joining the more than seven hundred lodges of Sioux friendlies who were already camped near the fort.

By now, Little Thunder had moved his people to a new campsite on Blue Water Creek four or five miles north of the North Platte River, some one hundred and forty miles east of Fort Laramie. Although the runners brought Little Thunder and his people the message to come in, they ignored it. They had just had a successful buffalo hunt and were busy preparing meat and curing hides for the winter ahead. Besides, everyone knew that Chief Little Thunder was a friendly. After all, he had been the one to talk the war-hungry young Sioux out of attacking Fort Laramie the night of the cow-trouble last year. He had saved the life of the trader, James Bordeaux, too, by helping to give out all his goods to the angry young warriors.

Now that same James Bordeaux was so concerned about the Brulés that he twice sent out runners to urge Little Thunder to come in with his people. But Little Thunder wouldn't consider it; certainly not before the buffalo meat had dried. As it turned out, Bordeaux knew something that Little Thunder didn't know. Or if Little Thunder knew it, he didn't take it seriously. General William Harney had been ordered to assemble a force of artillery, infantry and cavalry to march against the Sioux in retaliation for the cow-trouble, or what the whites called the Grattan Massacre.

Heading out from Fort Kearny in the Nebraska Territory,

Harney led more than five hundred men along the Oregon Trail. On his way to Fort Laramie, he learned that Little Thunder's camp was on Blue Water Creek, only a few miles north of his line of march. He immediately halted his men and made plans.

On the afternoon of September 3, 1855, Curly and four Brulé friends rode toward Little Thunder's camp under a threatening sky that had already begun to spit rain. They had been hunting and Curly was well pleased with his kill of a fat buckskin yearling. But as the five young hunters approached the canyon where their people were camped, they saw dark smoke rising above the sandstone bluffs. The smoke smelled, not of meat roasting or the sweet red willow bark of pipes being smoked, but of gunpowder and burning hides. Remembering Bordeaux's warnings, Curly's companions fled. But running off had never been Curly's way. If there was trouble, his people would need him.

Hobbling his ponies, Curly climbed to the top of a bluff that overlooked the Brulé camp. Thunderstruck, he saw that the village had been destroyed. The forty-some tipis were gone, fires smoldered where hides and meat had been torched, travois, parfleches, robes, blankets, clothing, saddles were scattered everywhere. Worst of all, not a person was to be seen. Quickly scouting around the edges of the camp, Curly found moccasin prints leading toward the northeast. But the prints had been trampled over by more prints, the prints of hard-heeled soldiers' boots.

Curly raced back to his pony, mounted and followed the trail. Not far from camp, at the foot of a sandstone bluff, Curly's pony snorted and shied. Curly hesitated, too. The rancid smell of gunpowder and blood was unmistakable. It was getting dark and as Curly urged his pony ahead, at first

35

he wasn't sure what he was looking at. Gradually, the forms took shape. Bodies were sprawled everywhere. Men, women, children and old ones had been killed, scalped, hacked and gashed beyond recognition. Many had been shot, others had been torn up by the exploding balls of the gun wagons.

The scene before him had nothing to do with warfare as Curly had ever known it: steal some horses, strike and kill a few of the enemy, count coup and ride hard for home. One or two dead in tribal warfare brought village-wide mourning, while five or six dead was a tribal disaster. Now Curly was confronted by a sight that no Sioux had ever seen before. Eighty-six of his people had been killed and mutilated.

Horrified as he was, Curly knew that he couldn't think of himself. Many of the Brulés were still missing. Somehow they must have escaped. By now it was raining and Curly hurriedly searched for tracks before they were washed away. There they were, moccasin prints, heading northeast toward the Sand Hills.

Curly hadn't ridden far when he heard the soft keening of a woman and the whimper of an infant. Following the sound, he pulled aside some low-hanging brush and found a Cheyenne woman hiding there, a newborn baby in her arms. Her name was Yellow Woman, she told Curly. She and her family had been visiting the Brulé camp at the time of the attack. Soldiers had killed her husband and young son back by the bluffs where they had all tried to hide. She had run with the others but had been forced to drop behind to give birth to her child.

Curly knew that helping this woman would slow him down. It was raining harder than ever and he was afraid that his people's tracks would be lost. Still, he knew that he couldn't abandon her. Riding back to the dark and terrible place where the bodies lay, Curly found an abandoned travois, strapped it onto his pony and returned to Yellow Woman. When he had settled Yellow Woman and her baby in the travois, he set out on foot, knowing that his pony was too worn out to carry him as well.

Only when Curly overtook what was left of Little Thunder's exhausted band some three or four miles beyond the sandstone bluffs did he learn what had happened.

The white-bearded general had sent a messenger to the Brulé camp under a white flag requesting a parley. After telling the women to pack up, Little Thunder, Spotted Tail and Iron Shell had ridden out a mile or so to meet with the soldier chief. Unarmed, they had parleyed in good faith, not knowing that Harney's cavalrymen had already positioned themselves to the rear of the Brulé camp to cut off any escape.

After half an hour of talk, Harney suddenly informed the three head men that he had come to fight and they had better be ready for war. Little Thunder, Spotted Tail and Iron Shell galloped back to camp to alert their people, most of whom had already struck their tipis and packed. Panicked, the Brulés left everything and fled toward what they thought would be the safety of the bluffs.

But the cavalrymen were there waiting with their big guns. It was a slaughter. Although Little Thunder and Spotted Tail courageously fought a rear guard action, they were both wounded, while seventy Brulé women and children, including Spotted Tail's young wife and baby daughter, were captured. Curly and everyone else knew what that meant. The women and children would be marched to Fort Laramie and locked up in the iron house that the whites called a jail. There they were sure to die.

Incredibly, even the destruction of Little Thunder's camp and the killing of his people in revenge for the death of Grattan and his men didn't satisfy Harney, whom the Sioux called White Beard. When he reached Fort Laramie with his prisoners, he announced that the yearly gifts of rations and goods, which had been guaranteed by the Horse Creek Treaty, would be given out only when the Brulés who had killed the three men on the mail wagon had surrendered. Until that time, war with the Sioux would continue.

For the next few weeks, Little Thunder and Spotted Tail, who were recovering from their wounds, helped the sorrowing Brulés establish a new camp. When the people were settled, a council was held and a decision made. Spotted Tail, Red Leaf and Long Chin, dressed in their finest ceremonial robes and singing their death songs, rode through the village. They were going to give themselves up to save their people.

Curly, along with other Brulé survivors, followed the three warriors to Fort Laramie in a display of support. What they saw was even worse than what they had expected. Spotted Tail, Red Leaf and Long Chin, bound in iron chains and balls, were ordered into an Army wagon to be driven east to Fort Kearny where they would be jailed with their women and children.

As the wagon carrying the three prisoners disappeared into the dust of the Holy Road, Curly silently folded his arms across his chest, rigid with anger. Although the Brulé women around him set up a great keening of grief, Curly remained silent. Better to die fighting . . . better to die fighting . . . better to die fighting . . .

CHAPTER 7

White Beard Harney still wasn't finished with the Sioux. The following year, in the Moon When the Grain Comes up, March, 1856, he ordered the Sioux chiefs to meet with him at Fort Pierre on the Missouri River. Alarmed at what had happened to the Brulés at Blue Water Creek, the head men braved the long journey through the snow and cold to attend the council.

At the meeting, they pledged to stop harassing emigrants on the Holy Road. They also gave permission for the whites to use an old fur traders' road that ran through the heart of their land from Fort Laramie to Fort Pierre, with the understanding that no whites would be allowed anywhere else in their territory. In exchange, White Beard Harney promised to once again hand out the annuities at Fort Laramie that he had stopped distributing four months before.

During the council, Harney decided to impress the chiefs with some of the white soldiers' magic. Chloroform had just come into use and Harney ordered the fort surgeon to give a stray dog a dose of chloroform and then amaze the chiefs by reviving it. The unconscious dog was passed around.

"Plenty dead," the chiefs agreed.

But try as he might, the surgeon couldn't revive the dog. He was indeed plenty dead.

"White man's medicine too strong," the amused chiefs pointed out.

Unlike the head men, Curly wanted nothing to do with the whites. For the next year and a half, he wandered restlessly from village to village. From the fall of 1856 to the summer of 1857, he lived south of the Platte River in Chief Black Kettle's Cheyenne camp, visiting Yellow Woman, the young mother whom he had rescued at Blue Water Creek. During the time that Curly was with the Cheyennes, the Cheyennes and the Army fought a few minor skirmishes, none of them serious.

The relative peace didn't last long. On July 29, 1857, scouts alerted Chief Black Kettle that a large force of soldiers was approaching. In an elaborate ceremony, the Cheyenne medicine man gave the warriors strong medicine to make them bulletproof. But much to the surprise of the Cheyennes, the soldiers didn't use their guns. Instead, they charged with their sabres. As the Cheyennes retreated in confusion, and the panicked people scattered, four Cheyenne warriors were killed. Although Curly fled with Yellow Woman and his Cheyenne friends, he stayed only long enough to help them get settled before leaving to ride north to Bear Butte to join his people.

Bear Butte was the Sioux' favorite gathering place, where they came together in late summer to trade gossip, see old friends and hold religious ceremonies. Although they roamed where the buffalo roamed and called no place home, Bear

Butte was special to the Sioux. And it was special to Curly, who had been born not far from Bear Butte in the fall of 1841 beside meandering Rapid Creek. Set in the middle of the open plains north of the Black Hills, from the south, Bear Butte looked like nothing so much as a sleeping bear. Curly's father, the holy man, Crazy Horse, had often preached to the people from Bear Butte's Teaching Hill. Now the people were assembling at the request of the head chiefs who had sent out sacred pipes to the seven Sioux tribes to come to Bear Butte for a great council.

It was a long journey to Bear Butte, but Curly had a lot to think about. After witnessing three battles, he had learned that no single village had the weapons or manpower to stand up to the Army. The one Sioux victory had been against Grattan and his men at the time of the cow-trouble, when hundreds and hundreds of Sioux warriors had joined together. It seemed that the only way to win against the soldiers was for the Sioux to unite in one great war party.

When Curly arrived at Bear Butte early in the Moon of the Ripe Plums, August, 1857, he was reassured not only by the sight of the huge sleeping bear that was Bear Butte, but also by the thousands of Sioux camped around the base of the butte for many miles. This was a homecoming for Curly and it didn't take him long to find the Oglala camp where he was reunited with his parents, sister and brother, Little Hawk, who was already known to be a reckless risk-taker.

Curly's best friend, his *kola,* Hump, was there, too, as well as Young-Man-Afraid-of-His-Horses, He Dog and Lone Bear, the one who could always make them laugh. And for the first time Curly came to know his seven-foot-tall Miniconjou cousin, Touch-the-Clouds, and before long the two were good friends.

Everyone at Bear Butte was aware of how much Curly had

41

changed. He wasn't as tall as the other sixteen-year-olds, and never would be, but he had been many places and seen much, and what he had experienced gave him an air of strength and authority. Although his hair and skin were still pale, his face was leaner. One of his friends, Short Bull, later said that Curly's "features were not like those of the rest of us. His face was not broad, and he had a sharp, high nose. He had black eyes that hardly ever looked straight at a man, but they didn't miss much that was going on all the same."

More than five thousand Sioux had already arrived at Bear Butte and set up their circles of tipis. The Oglalas, Hunkpapas, Sans Arcs, Miniconjous, Two Kettles and Blackfeet-Sioux were all there with their head men, warrior-chiefs whom Curly had long heard about. Only the Brulés were missing. Although Spotted Tail, Red Leaf and Long Chin and their women and children had been released from jail, the Brulés had suffered enough. They had refused to come to the council, declaring that they would no longer wage war against the whites.

It had been a long time since there had been such a Sioux gathering and there was feasting, singing and dancing well into the nights. Everyone had a wonderful time. Old men got together to smoke their pipes and relive ancient battles, women gossiped and children played their games, while older boys and girls courted. Although Curly was too young for marriage, Black Buffalo Woman, Chief Red Cloud's niece, attracted his attention and his eyes turned her way often. And when she thought he wasn't looking, Black Buffalo Woman's eyes turned toward him.

As for the head chiefs, they were well pleased as they looked around and saw how many they were and how powerful. It had been a mistake, they now admitted, to have given

42

in to the soldier-chief White Beard's demands without a fight. They would never again cave in so easily. From now on, the Sioux would join together in a united front against any whites who dared to try to take their land.

During the council meetings, the chiefs smoked their sacred pipes, made promises to one another and pledged solemn vows. But the freedom and independence of each individual, which was so valued by the Sioux, worked against them in wartime. The Sioux, who fought battles, not wars, were best at hit-and-run raids, harassment and guerilla tactics, as well as using their surroundings for their own advantage and their enemies' disadvantage. Except when they were taken by surprise, or when their families were in danger, they fought only on their own terms and when victory seemed certain.

After the young men had completed their Sun Dance, the council broke up and the people went their separate ways, filled with optimism and hope for the future. But no long-range plans had been made. No commander-in-chief had been appointed, scouts weren't organized, no communication system between tribes had been set up, the question of acquiring guns and ammunition hadn't been considered and no decision had been made as to when or how they would take a stand.

It was true that the talk had been good, that uniting together was their one hope. But talk was only words and words had never won a battle.

CHAPTER 8

After the council at Bear Butte broke up and the people had left, Curly and his father rode off alone so that Crazy Horse could instruct his son on his responsibilities as a warrior. On a high place, overlooking the stream where Curly had been born, they constructed a sweat lodge of willow poles and covered the frame with robes to make it airtight. After they built a fire, they dug a shallow pit in the center of the sweat lodge and placed hot rocks from the fire in the pit. They then threw cold water over the rocks to produce great clouds of steam. Naked, Crazy Horse and Curly entered the sweat lodge to purify themselves in the scalding steam. Once they were purified, Crazy Horse schooled Curly in his future duties and responsibilities.

There were four virtues that all Sioux men must strive for, Crazy Horse said. Bravery was the first. It went without saying that Curly was to be brave in all matters. Crazy Horse recited an old Sioux saying that Curly had heard before, "It is better to die on the battlefield than to live to be old." Fortitude was the next virtue. Curly was to endure physical pain, hunger and thirst without complaint. He was also to handle his personal relationships with reserve, consideration and dignity. Generosity was the third virtue. Curly was always to provide for the helpless ones. Again, Crazy Horse repeated a tribal saying, "A man must help others as much as possible, no matter who, by giving him horses, food or clothing." The last virtue, wisdom, was the highest, and the hardest, to attain. Wisdom was a way of life. Curly was to deny himself in the giving of his personal energies to the well-being of others. He was to get along with his people, to lead, to advise, to settle disputes and to inspire.

As they talked, Curly decided that now was the time to tell his father of his vision. If he waited much longer, the memory of it might fade. When Curly had finished speaking, Crazy Horse was silent for a long time. Finally, as a holy man, he interpreted his son's vision.

You must do as the man in your vision told you and dress as he was dressed, Crazy Horse said. You must wear a single hawk feather in your hair and a stone behind your ear, paint a streak of lightning on your face and hail spots on your body. Throw dust over yourself and your pony before you fight and be sure never to take anything from a battle for yourself. If you hold true to these charges, no weapon can harm you. But your vision has placed a great burden on you as a leader of your people and you must always be faithful to it.

It was soon after Curly's talk with his father that his time of testing as an Oglala warrior came. For the first time since the Sioux had arrived on the Great Plains in the 1700s, the buffalo herds had moved out of the Oglalas' hunting range into the Powder River country far to the west. It was the land of the Sioux' enemies, the Crows, the Arapahoes and the Shoshonis, known to the Sioux as the Snakes. The Oglalas had a choice. They could return to Fort Laramie and the Holy Road and live on handouts from the whites as Laramie Loafers. Or they could follow the buffalo west into the Powder River country and wage war on their enemies.

For Curly, it wasn't much of a choice. He would never become a Loafer and live on what the whites chose to give him. After all, he was not only a warrior, but a warrior with powerful medicine. Furthermore, successful warfare brought prestige and honor to a warrior, raised him to a leadership position, earned him a wife and gained him membership in a warrior society. "When we were young all we thought about was going to war with some other nation," Curly's friend, the medicine man, Chips, recalled. "All tried to get their names up the highest, and whoever did so was the principal man in the nation; and Crazy Horse [Curly] wanted to get to the highest station and rank."

Warfare it would be. Late in the summer of 1858, Curly, his brother, Little Hawk, his *kola,* Hump, Lone Bear and a number of other young warriors prepared to ride west into the Powder River country. The night before they left, the people beat their drums, danced and sang strong-heart songs to empower the warriors. The next morning, the war party rode through camp, the men leading their trained war ponies on a lariat and carrying their weapons, as well as cases holding their shields, war clothes, war bonnets, war paint, pipes and tobacco, extra moccasins and dried food for the journey ahead. As each warrior passed through the lines of people on his way out of camp, the women made the trilling sound and called out his name.

The war party rode west under Hump, farther west than

46

any Oglala had ever been before, all the way to the Arapaho and Shoshoni territory of Wind River. After days of travel, one of the scouts came back to report that he had found an Arapaho camp with many fine ponies. Although the Oglalas had never seen an Arapaho, knew nothing about them and didn't understand their language, they were sure that they could defeat them in warfare.

The Oglala warriors readied themselves. To seek protection and success in battle, they took their war clothes from their cases, shook them to the sky, the earth and the four directions. They made their medicine and sang their sacred war songs. Some of them put on fine buckskin shirts and leggings, quilled arm bands or bone breast plates. Most, however, stripped down to their breechcloths and moccasins. They tied up their hair and painted their faces and bodies, as well as their war ponies. After knotting their ponies' tails, they took their shields from their covers, shook loose their ornaments and hung them on their left arms. Then they armed themselves.

For the first time, Curly prepared himself as he had been instructed in his vision. He already wore a small stone behind his ear that Chips had given him. Now he placed a single hawk feather in his scalp lock, painted a lightning streak from his forehead to his chin, dotted his body with a number of hail spots and threw dust over both himself and his war pony. He was as ready as he would ever be.

But the Arapahoes had scouts, too, and they had sighted the approaching Oglalas. As Hump led the Oglala war party toward the enemy camp, the Arapaho warriors, who were hidden behind rocks on a high hill, opened fire. The surprised Oglalas quickly circled out of range, regrouped and then charged. They shot at the Arapahoes from under the necks of

47

their ponies with only their feet showing to the enemy. But the Arapahoes were well protected on their hillside position and the Oglalas couldn't dislodge them.

The fighting had already gone on for two hours when Curly's pony was hit and went down. Leaping off, Curly grabbed a riderless pony, mounted and rode up the hill amid flying bullets and arrows. He counted three coups before he turned and galloped back down, whooping and hollering as he came. The Oglalas at the bottom of the hill shouted out his name in honor of his bravery.

But counting coup wasn't enough for Curly. With the Arapahoes concentrating all their fire on him, he charged back up the hill. Like the man in his vision, he rode untouched through another barrage of bullets and arrows. Stretched out low on the back of his pony, he killed an Arapaho warrior with a single arrow, jumped his pony over the dead man, turned and killed a second Arapaho. Dismounting, Curly hastily scalped the first man, but just as he lifted the scalp from the second man, an enemy arrow slammed into his leg. At the searing pain, Curly let go of his pony and the animal galloped away.

With his comrades calling out his name over and over, Curly raced back down the hill on foot as fast as he could. All the time that Hump was removing the arrow and dressing the wound, Curly was scolding himself. The man in his vision had told him never to take anything from a battle and he had taken two scalps. What a foolish gesture! No wonder he had lost his power and been wounded. He threw away the scalps in disgust.

The night after the Oglala war party arrived back in camp with scalps, fine new ponies and no men missing or killed, there was a scalp dance performed by the warriors' mothers

48

and sisters. The people celebrated with a great feast as well. At the feast, each warrior stood and sang of his own heroism, of his courage in battle, of the fine ponies he had stolen and the coups he had counted. At the end of each recital, everyone cheered. They expected their warriors to boast. If they didn't boast, they would never receive the praise and honor that they deserved.

Even though he was now a man-warrior, Curly, at seventeen, didn't care for such public boasting and the emotional outcries that greeted it, at least for himself. Twice he was pushed forward into the circle and urged to sing of his own brave deeds and twice he refused. But others described how Curly had killed two enemy warriors and how his strong medicine had allowed him to ride unharmed through bullets and arrows. Everyone present knew of Curly's thoughtful, quiet ways. Now they knew of his courage and daring as well.

The next morning, Crazy Horse braided his long hair with fur, took his sacred pipe from its pouch and put on his best ceremonial blanket, the one with the handsome beadwork that told the story of his own vision. With his blanket held around him, Crazy Horse walked slowly and proudly through the village singing a song of a new name for his son.

My son has been against the people of unknown tongue.
He has done a brave thing;
For this I give him a new name, the name of his father,
and of many fathers before him—
I give him a great name.
I call him Crazy Horse.

CHAPTER 9

When Curly was a boy, he and his family had camped near Fort Laramie during the summers because the head man of their Oglala band had dearly loved his coffee and tobacco. There, Curly had watched the Sioux become dependent on government handouts and traders' goods. And he had seen the traders' whiskey turn his camp into a battleground. He saw, too, how many of the Oglala women who married white fur trappers, traders and even soldiers, were left with children to raise alone after the men moved on. Even worse were the white man's diseases of smallpox, measles, cholera and tuberculosis that killed thousands of the Plains peoples.

Before the coming of the whites, life had been very different for the Sioux, whose name came from the French word "Nadouessioux," meaning "adders" or "enemies." The Sioux Nation had originally been made up of Seven Council Fires. Four of the Council Fires had merged into the Santee Sioux, or the Dakota, who settled on the eastern plains of

Minnesota. Two Council Fires, the Yankton and the Yanktonais Sioux, or the Nakota, settled more or less permanently in the central plains of the Missouri River Valley.

The largest of the Council Fires, the Teton Sioux, became nomadic buffalo hunters living on the Great Plains. Although the correct name for the Teton Sioux was Lakota, over time Sioux became the name commonly used. (The seven tribes of the Teton Sioux were the Oglalas, Brulés, Hunkpapas, Miniconjous, Sans Arcs, Two Kettles and Blackfeet-Sioux.) It was these Teton Sioux who controlled the land between the Missouri River Valley and eastern Wyoming and between the North Platte River and the Yellowstone River.

Now, in 1858, the Oglalas were fighting for more land to the west, the Powder River country of their enemies, the Crows and Shoshonis. Curly, now known as Crazy Horse (his father took the name Worm), stayed north with his people, far from Fort Laramie and any whites. In a campaign to seize the Powder River country, he joined war parties, along with his brother, Little Hawk, and his friends, to ride against their enemies. They stole enemy horses, counted coups, brought back scalps (all but Crazy Horse) and won honors for themselves. It wasn't long before the Oglala war parties had pushed the Crows and Shoshonis all the way back to the Bighorn Mountains. The Powder River country was theirs!

Stretching west from the Black Hills to the Bighorn Mountains, the Powder River country abounded in game almost beyond imagining, with herds of buffalo blanketing the earth, elk, deer, bear, antelope and game birds by the millions. Oglala ponies grew fat on an endless supply of rich grass, while wooded valleys and fresh streams provided shelter and water for winter camping.

As the years passed, Crazy Horse became an expert hunter.

51

With both his vision and his father's advice in mind, he kept only as much for himself as he needed, sharing the rest with those who had no one to provide for them. He even gave away the ponies that he stole from the Crows and Shoshonis.

Just as Crazy Horse often hunted alone, he often acted alone in battle, too. Sometimes he worked as a decoy to lead the enemy toward the main body of Oglala warriors. At other times, he dropped behind to divert the enemy and give his war party time to get away.

Soon Crazy Horse became known as a warrior who would never leave a wounded comrade on the field of battle, or the body of a dead one to be scalped, either. The other warriors were eager to join any war party that Crazy Horse was going on. And everyone knew that Crazy Horse's medicine was powerful, especially since the medicine man, Chips, gave him a small white stone that he wore on a thong over his shoulder and under his left arm to ward off danger. Crazy Horse's friend He Dog said later, "Crazy Horse always led his men himself when they went into battle, and he kept well in front of them. He headed many charges . . . He always tried to kill as many as possible of the enemy without losing his own men."

Because of his growing reputation as a warrior, Crazy Horse was invited to join an *akicita* society, the Crow Owners. Like all *akicita* societies, the Crow Owners kept order in the camp, guarded the people when they were on the move and reined in young warriors from riding out and spoiling an enemy raid or a buffalo surround. The Crow Owners had their own lodge away from the women, where they could smoke their pipes, entertain one another with tales of their courageous deeds, gossip, sing, dance and tell rough jokes. Although Crazy Horse didn't spend much time in their lodge, he joined the Crow Owners on hunts and war parties.

One of the few times that Crazy Horse was in close-to-death danger was in the summer of 1861 on a raid against the Shoshonis. Taking the Shoshoni village by surprise, the Oglala war party made off with a herd of at least four hundred ponies. As the Shoshonis rode after them in hot pursuit, Crazy Horse, Little Hawk, and six or seven others dropped behind in a delaying action to give their comrades time to get away.

With Little Hawk at his side, Crazy Horse had his men ride a good distance, dismount, hide behind some rocks and fire arrows at the pursuing Shoshonis. When the enemy bore down on them, Crazy Horse and his men mounted, rode for another short stretch and repeated the maneuver. But for once, Crazy Horse misjudged the distance between his decoy party and the enemy. As the Shoshonis quickly surrounded them in overwhelming numbers, an enemy arrow felled Crazy Horse's pony. Moments later, Little Hawk's pony went down, too, and all of a sudden, Crazy Horse and Little Hawk found themselves on foot and alone. Although the two brothers fought fiercely they knew that they couldn't hold off the Shoshonis indefinitely. Sure enough, two Shoshoni warriors broke rank and galloped toward them.

"Take care of yourself—I'll do the fancy stunt," Crazy Horse called to Little Hawk.

With that, Crazy Horse stepped in the path of the charging Shoshoni and moved as if to dodge to his right. As the Shoshoni turned to ride him down, Crazy Horse leapt to the left, grabbed the Shoshoni's leg as he passed and unseated him. Quickly mounting the riderless pony, Crazy Horse glanced around for Little Hawk. He had knocked the other Shoshoni off his pony with an arrow and he, too, was mounted. As Crazy Horse and Little Hawk rode safely away together, the sound of their laughter trailed behind them.

There was no doubt about it. Those years when Crazy

Horse was growing into manhood were the best of times. They were good not only for Crazy Horse, but also for all those Oglalas who lived free of the whites in their newly won Powder River country.

CHAPTER 10

Crazy Horse was in love. He had known, and fancied, Black Buffalo Woman ever since they had been in their teen years. Now that he was twenty-one, marriage was very much on his mind and he began to court her.

At dusk, Crazy Horse would stand outside of Black Buffalo Woman's tipi until she recognized his presence by stepping out. After enfolding Black Buffalo Woman in his blanket, Crazy Horse made sure that their heads were covered so that they could talk privately face to face. But their time together was always short. Because other young men came courting Black Buffalo Woman, there were always suitors lined up with their blankets outside her tipi and Crazy Horse had to wait his turn. With young Sioux women strictly chaperoned, Crazy Horse had almost no opportunity to be alone with Black Buffalo Woman. A casual meeting on the water path, a smile, a nod or a meaningful look at a dance or celebration was about the best he could do.

Although Crazy Horse sensed that Black Buffalo Woman was attracted to him, he couldn't be sure what his chances were. Despite the prestige he had earned as a warrior, hunter and member of the Crow Owners *akicita* society, he was in the Hunkpatila band of Oglalas and Black Buffalo Woman was in the Bad Face band. Furthermore, her family was far more prominent than his. While Crazy Horse's father was a humble holy man, Black Buffalo Woman's uncle was the great Bad Face chief, Red Cloud. And it didn't help that Crazy Horse's main rival was No Water, whose brother was a leader in Red Cloud's council.

Early in the summer of 1862, at a time when Crazy Horse was visiting in Black Buffalo Woman's Bad Face village, Chief Red Cloud announced plans for a grand war party against the Crows. Crazy Horse prepared to go, as did Little Hawk and his friends, Hump, Lone Bear, He Dog . . . and No Water. But on the morning they were to leave, No Water sat on the ground rocking back and forth in agony with a toothache. Since No Water's medicine was the two fierce teeth of a grizzly bear, no one questioned his decision to stay home.

Hou! Crazy Horse and his friends had a glorious two weeks. They took one scalp, counted coups, stole many ponies and made off with Crow ceremonial shirts, war bonnets and guns. Best of all, not one Oglala was even wounded. Although Crazy Horse was his usual quiet self on the way home, the others joked, told stories and sang songs of their daring and bravery to make the long journey pass more quickly.

As they approached the Bad Face village, the young man called Woman's Dress, who was a *winkte*, hurried out to meet them. (The Sioux believed that *winkte*s, or homosexuals, had special powers to foretell the future.) This day, however,

Woman's Dress had news of something that had already happened. Pulling Crazy Horse aside, he announced that while the war party had been gone, Black Buffalo Woman had married No Water.

Crazy Horse was stunned. The woman he loved had married somebody else. It couldn't be! Immediately he left Red Cloud's village and headed for home. There, instead of going up on a hilltop to sing out his grief to the sky as was customary in times of sorrow, he retreated into his family's lodge where he stayed for three days without speaking. When he came out, he silently packed, saddled his pony and rode off, trailing his war pony behind him. He didn't return for two months. Crazy Horse never spoke of where he had gone or what he had done. He simply tossed two Crow scalps to the dogs, the only scalps he had taken in four years of fighting.

CHAPTER 11

Crazy Horse stayed north in the Powder River country for the next two years. Far from any whites, he staged raids on the Crows and Shoshonis, continued his solitary hunting and occasionally traveled south to visit the Southern Oglalas and the Cheyennes.

Although Crazy Horse had many friends, Hump, Lone Bear, He Dog, Little Big Man and Young-Man-Afraid-of-His-Horses, in 1863 he made a new and unlikely friend, a white soldier, Caspar Collins. Stationed at Fort Laramie where his father was commander, Lieutenant Caspar Collins was interested in everything about the Sioux, their beliefs, their customs, their language. Traveling alone, he often stopped at Sioux villages where he came to know the Sioux as people rather than as "red men." (Because they painted their faces with red paint mixed with grease to prevent sun and wind burn, the Plains peoples were often called red men.)

Collins spent most of the winter of 1863 in Crazy Horse's

winter camp where Crazy Horse taught him the language, explained Sioux rituals and practices, showed him how to make a bow and arrows and took him on hunts. By the time Collins left the Powder River country in the spring of 1864, he and Crazy Horse considered themselves friends.

Crazy Horse also left the Powder River country that spring of 1864. Black Buffalo Woman had a new infant son and seeing the woman he loved with a husband and child may have been too painful for him. Or he may have left because he craved new adventure and more war honors. Whatever the reason, Crazy Horse rode south to the Platte River on his favorite bay that he had stolen from the Crows to join the Southern Oglalas, the Cheyennes and the Arapahoes, who were now allies, in raids against the whites.

Although the old chiefs did their best to keep the peace, hot-blooded young warriors, like Crazy Horse, couldn't be held back. Plundering white settlements, isolated outposts and especially wagon trains along the Holy Road yielded far more loot, with far less danger, than warring against the Crows and Shoshonis. More important, these whites had to be driven out of what had never been, and must never be, their land.

With the Civil War raging back east during the years 1861 to 1865, only a handful of soldiers could be spared for the frontier, far too few to put a stop to the hostiles' hit-and-run raids. Despite the shortage of soldiers, every so often, a superior officer was sent west and Colonel William Collins was one of those. Much of what Colonel Collins knew about the Plains tribes he had learned from his son, Crazy Horse's friend, Lieutenant Caspar Collins.

Aware that his first duty was to keep the peace, Colonel Collins worked hard to curb his men who were itching for a showdown with the "savages." Collins realized, too, that the old chiefs were having the same problem keeping their young daredevils under control that he was. A decent and humane man, Collins also understood the reasons for the Plains tribes' anger—the unprovoked attacks on innocent villages, the broken treaties, the ruined hunting grounds, the takeover of their land and the whites' diseases that had killed so many of their people.

And it was true that the Plains tribes were angry, very angry. Just as the whites broke treaties, the Plains tribes broke treaties, too. Adopting their usual tactics, Crazy Horse and his friend, Little Big Man, along with small bands of Southern Oglalas, Southern Cheyennes and Arapahoes, stormed supply depots, stagecoach stations, ranches, telegraph offices, stagecoaches, wagon trains and freight wagons, stealing, burning and killing all along the Platte River. They pulled down telegraph poles and wires and stole cattle, mules and livestock. They especially prized the soldiers' big American horses, which lacked the long-distance stamina of their ponies but which were much larger and faster. Billy Garnett, an interpreter, whose mother had been a Sioux, commented: "Crazy Horse and Little Big Man were very harassing on the Platte. They carried on a lively business of horse-stealing and the killing of white men."

Although the terrorized whites might not have believed it, there were many Sioux and Cheyennes who wanted no part of war. In the fall of 1864, a friendly band of Cheyennes under Chief Black Kettle asked the Army for protection. When they were told to move to Sand Creek in Kansas where their safety would be guaranteed, the seven hundred or more Cheyennes accepted the offer and set up camp. At dawn on November 29, 1864, a large body of soldiers was seen marching toward Sand Creek. Black Kettle quickly ran up an American flag, with a white flag under it, to indicate that his camp was friendly. The flags made no difference. The soldiers attacked, killing, scalping and mutilating some 150 Cheyennes, most of whom were women and children.

Enraged, those Cheyennes who survived immediately sent their pipe bearers around to all their allies with a red-feathered war pipe. (A white-feathered pipe meant peace.) The leaders of more than eight hundred lodges of Southern Oglalas, Brulés and Arapahoes smoked the pipe to indicate that they would join the Cheyennes in waging war. As for Crazy Horse, he hankered for revenge. He had not only spent almost a year in Black Kettle's village and had come to know the people well, but his special friend, Yellow Woman, whom he had rescued from the Blue Water Creek massacre nine years before, had also been one of those killed.

Although war parties seldom went out in the winter, the warriors were so inflamed by the slaughter that they didn't wait for warmer weather. In the Moon of the Trees Popping, January, 1865, a war party of at least a thousand Sioux, Cheyennes and Arapahoes, including Crazy Horse and Little Big Man, headed for Julesburg in the Colorado Territory to avenge the Sand Creek massacre. The women came, too, along with pack ponies to bring back the plunder. The Sioux led the march. They knew the way and besides, they had smoked the war pipe first and custom dictated that they be given the lead.

After attacking a stagecoach on the Julesburg road, the war party's next target was Camp Rankin (later Fort Sedgwick), just west of Julesburg. A small decoy party rode out to lure the soldiers into the open. But when the cavalry gave chase and began firing at the decoys, the impatient warriors gave a yell of triumph and rode out of hiding. At the sight of a thousand mounted warriors, the cavalry beat a fast retreat back into their stockade, but not before they had lost fourteen men.

After they had scalped the fourteen soldiers, the war party attacked and plundered the Julesburg stagecoach station, blacksmith shop, store and warehouse. They took boots, shoes, hardware, clothing, bolts of calico and silk, sacks of flour, corn meal, rice, sugar, coffee, crates of hams and bacon, boxes of dried fruit and tins of oysters. (They especially loved the oysters.) For the next six days, the warriors burned ranches in the surrounding countryside, captured wagon trains and ran off cattle. Meanwhile, their women set up camp on the north bank of the South Platte River, an enormous village of many hundreds of lodges.

For the next month, Crazy Horse and Little Big Man rode with Sioux and Cheyenne war parties, raiding the South Platte River valley so fiercely that they soon regained control of the whole area. Because the war parties were often out at night, the women kept huge beacon fires burning in the camp that could be seen for many miles up and down the Platte River. If the beacon fires weren't visible, the war parties would find their way back by following the beat of the drums that throbbed throughout the nights for the scalp dances. On February 2, 1865, while the women were packing up the camp to move on, the warriors again attacked Julesburg, taking anything that was still left and setting fire to all the buildings.

Again the old Sioux chiefs led the way as they knew the best routes and camping sites. When the huge village, which moved north in a column that was a mile or more wide, reached a good campsite, the chiefs would dismount and direct the crier to call out, "Camp here." At the order, the women would unpack and put up their tipis. If they were only to stay overnight, the crier would shout out, "Camp here, one sleep." The women would then unpack only a few necessities.

The great mass of men, women and children, with their belongings, as well as enormous amounts of loot and huge pony herds, captured horses, cattle and mules, moved across the Sand Hills to the Black Hills. From there they traveled north and west to the Powder River over some of the most difficult terrain in the country. Their four-hundred-mile journey through the howling winds and beating snow of a harsh Plains winter was an incredible feat.

Arriving in the Powder River country, Crazy Horse, with the Oglalas and Northern Cheyennes, headed for the winter village of the Oglalas. When the Oglala warriors who were camped there heard about the Sand Creek massacre and saw all the booty that Crazy Horse and the others had plundered, they decided that they, too, would go on the warpath come spring. With that decision, any possibility of peace that might still have existed between the Powder River Oglalas and the whites was ended for good.

CHAPTER 12

With the Civil War over in the spring of 1865, all new Army officers were sent west, including a replacement for Colonel Collins. Unlike Colonel Collins, the new officers, for the most part, viewed the Plains tribes as just another enemy force to fight . . . and conquer.

In the Moon of the Ripe Juneberries, June, a white woman, Mrs. Eubanks, who had been captured the year before, was brought into Fort Laramie by two Oglala chiefs. They had bought her from the Cheyennes at great trouble and expense. When the hysterical Mrs. Eubanks claimed that the two chiefs had tortured her, the officer in charge of Fort Laramie never thought to question why the Oglalas would personally bring in a captive whom they had abused. Instead, he ordered that both chiefs be hanged with iron balls on their legs and their bodies guarded so that their people couldn't take them down for a decent burial. To the horror of the Fort Laramie friendlies, the two blackened bodies swung in the wind until their legs dropped off from the weight of the iron balls. (Death by hanging held a special terror for the Sioux as they believed that the person's spirit could never leave his body.)

The Fort Laramie friendlies soon got another taste of white man's justice. When the newly appointed commander of the whole military district heard how many Sioux friendlies were camped around Fort Laramie, he demanded to know why they hadn't been attacked. They were friendlies, he was told, living on government rations and annuities under the protection of the Army according to the 1851 Horse Creek Treaty. The commander wouldn't hear of it. They must all be moved to Fort Kearny, he ordered.

By this time, Crazy Horse's Brulé uncle, Spotted Tail, had come in and was camped at Fort Laramie. During his time in jail, he had taken a hard look at the sheer number of Americans as well as their military power. Ever since his release from jail, he had worked for peace and in the Moon of the Birth of Calves, April, 1865, he and Chief Little Thunder had brought 185 Brulé lodges into Fort Laramie as friendlies. But when Spotted Tail heard of the order to move to Fort Kearny, he protested. Fort Kearny was in Pawnee country and Pawnees were the Sioux' mortal enemies, he explained. With the Army having taken all the friendlies' guns and ponies, the Pawnees would slaughter them.

It didn't matter. The new commander of Fort Laramie, Colonel Thomas Moonlight, ordered the more than fifteen hundred Fort Laramie friendlies to pack up their belongings. On June 11, 1865, they started out for Fort Kearny under guard.

Eating the dust of wagon wheels, the old, the sick and the helpless ones were forced to keep up a relentless pace during

65

the first few days of march. If any of the young boys were caught misbehaving, the soldiers threatened to tie them to the wagon wheels and whip them. Some of the soldiers made a sport of throwing small children into the North Platte River and laughing as they struggled to swim out, while others took young Sioux women into their camp at night.

When the Oglala hostiles got word of the forced march, they made plans for a rescue. Knowing that the friendlies were camped on the west bank of Horse Creek, Crazy Horse snuck in after dark and contacted Spotted Tail and the other head men. Their people were on the other side of the river, ready to help, he told them. Ponies and arms were waiting.

On June 14, at dawn, an Army captain, accompanied by only a few soldiers, rode into the friendlies' camp to see why they hadn't started to move out. In the middle of his fiery tirade, a young warrior shot and killed the officer. As the other soldiers fled in panic, the friendlies raced for the North Platte River, leaving all their belongings behind. The hostiles had driven stakes into the river bottom at a spot where it was shallow enough to cross on foot. As the people waded to the other side and picked up the ponies that were waiting for them, the Oglala warriors stood guard. Everyone escaped except for a friendly who was riding in a wagon with a ball and chain on his leg. In their fury, the soldiers killed and scalped him.

In just one month, the Army had hanged two Oglala chiefs without a trial or even an inquiry and had made the senseless decision to move the friendlies to Fort Kearny. By doing so, the military had managed to turn fifteen hundred friendlies, including Spotted Tail, into fifteen hundred angry hostiles.

When Colonel Moonlight, who had been on a wild goose chase pursuing Sioux and Cheyennes to the west, heard about the escape, he was furious. Although he had no idea where the Oglalas and the rescued friendlies were headed, he rounded up every available cavalryman he could find and started out after them. Some eighty miles from Fort Laramie, Moonlight had his men turn their horses loose to graze despite warnings from his Crow scouts that the horses shouldn't be left unguarded.

That night, Crazy Horse, with several other braves, swept into the soldiers' camp, shouting and yelling and waving buffalo blankets to stampede the horses in their standard horse-stealing tactics. Within minutes, Crazy Horse and his party had made off with the whole herd. Even better than acquiring the big American horses was the pleasure of knowing that Moonlight and his men would have to walk the eighty miles back to Fort Laramie through rough, waterless terrain, carrying their saddles and equipment the whole way.

As Crazy Horse and the other Oglala warriors led the huge encampment of once-friendly, now-hostile, Sioux to the Powder River country, the Oglala head men there were meeting in council. The time had come to work together with other Sioux tribes to stop the white invasion by launching a full-scale attack, they agreed.

Sioux bravery and daring were never in question. What was in question was whether or not the hotheaded young warriors would be willing to put aside their quest for personal honor and prestige to wage war with a disciplined and united front.

CHAPTER 13

Crazy Horse was there when it all came together in the Moon of the Ripening Chokecherries, July, 1865, plans for a great Sioux and Cheyenne expedition against the whites. This expedition was no quick strike but a well-thought-out two-pronged attack. Runners had carried messages between the Oglalas on the Powder River and the far north country where Sitting Bull and his Hunkpapas were camped. While the Oglalas and the Cheyennes were attacking the Holy Road at the Platte Bridge, Sitting Bull's Hunkpapas would be striking Fort Rice on the northern Missouri River. A successful double offensive would cut off all communication between the whites.

Crazy Horse was twenty-four now, at his peak as a hunter and a warrior. A little below medium height and slightly built, he was about five feet eight inches tall and weighed around 140 pounds. Even though his coloring had darkened somewhat, his skin was still noticeably lighter than his companions' and so was his hair, which he usually wore in braids that hung below his belt. The Oglala warrior, Red Feather, later said, "Crazy Horse was a nice-looking man, with brown—not black hair, a sharp nose, and a narrow face . . . His nose was straight and thin. His hair was very long, straight, and fine in texture."

As usual, Crazy Horse's preparations for the coming battle took almost no time at all. He wore what his vision dictated, breechcloth and moccasins, a hawk feather in his hair and one stone behind his ear with another under his left arm. His war paint was still a single lightning streak down his cheek and a few hail spots on his body. Because eight ponies had been shot out from under him, Chips, the medicine man, had given Crazy Horse a stone to tie in his favorite bay's tail for protection.

Unlike Crazy Horse, the other warriors took days to prepare. For this, their first big, united offensive, they went to the old chiefs to learn the sacred ways, the words to ancient war songs, what to take and what to wear. For potent new medicine, they kept Chips busy.

The warriors took great pains with every detail of their gear, packing up their war bonnets, war shirts, lances, war clubs, bows and arrows and shields, as well as guns, if they had them. Important to their sense of self were the elaborate and unique designs that they painted on their faces and bodies so that they might be recognized during the battle and admired for their brave deeds. Even their ponies had special paint to protect them.

Ready at last, with their ponies decorated with eagle feathers (all but Crazy Horse's), the three thousand warriors held parades within their own tipi circles, singing the old war songs. To the acclaim of the people, they headed out of the vast camp and started up the Powder River. *Akicita* outriders guarded them on all sides to prevent any excited young warrior from breaking away to win honors on his own.

The Oglala chiefs, Red Cloud and Man-Afraid-of-His-Horses, and the Cheyenne chief, Roman Nose, carried the war pipes at the head of the procession that was made up mostly of Oglalas and Cheyennes but included Northern Arapahoes, Brulés, Miniconjous and Sans Arcs as well. Neither Crazy Horse nor any of the other warriors had ever seen such a large and colorful war party, and after the success of their raids along the South Platte River the year before, they were confident of victory.

Three days of marching brought the huge force to the Platte Bridge where the Holy Road crossed the North Platte River. As they drew near, they rode their ponies slowly so as not to raise a cloud of dust that would give their whereabouts away. Although the Platte Bridge Station (later known as Fort Caspar) had been built to defend the bridge, the head men didn't consider the few soldiers posted there to be a threat, not with the plan of attack that they had worked out. While the main body of men remained hidden, Crazy Horse would lead a decoy party down to the garrison to entice the soldiers into leaving their stockade. Once the soldiers were in the open, the war party would ride out of hiding and easily overwhelm them.

At dawn on July 25, 1865, Crazy Horse threw some dust over both himself and his bay. As the warriors concealed themselves in the surrounding hills, Crazy Horse and his decoy party of twenty men mounted and rode toward the Platte Bridge. As they drew near, they shouted and flapped their buffalo blankets as if to stampede the Army's herd of horses. When a company of cavalrymen came hurrying out of

70

the fort with a howitzer, Crazy Horse and the others put on a show of pretending to retreat so that the soldiers would be goaded into following. When they didn't set out in pursuit, Crazy Horse and a Cheyenne warrior fired several shots into their midst. The soldiers, in turn, lobbed a few howitzer shells back.

The sound of shooting was too much for the waiting warriors. First one and then another made it past the *akicita* guards and galloped to the crest of the hill to see what was happening. Within minutes, the whole war party had broken rank. One look at some three thousand mounted warriors in full war regalia poised on the nearby hills and the soldiers hightailed it back to their stockade.

The head men were furious that the trap had been ruined. After they had the *akicita* guards round up the warriors, they sent High Backed Wolf, a Cheyenne, to ride down and order the decoy party to return. But the decoy party refused.

"Now, when I see anything and go to get it, I want to succeed in getting it," one of the Oglala decoys replied angrily and Crazy Horse shouted his agreement. After all, they had come to fight, hadn't they?

High Backed Wolf tried to talk them into returning. "All right, I feel just as you do about that, but I am trying to do what the head men have asked me to do," he said. Then, at the possibility of a good fight, he changed his mind. "Come on now, let us swim the river and get close to the soldiers." With a war cry, Crazy Horse, High Backed Wolf and the others plunged their ponies into the river and swam across.

In the skirmish that followed, High Backed Wolf was shot and killed. (Although the Cheyenne medicine man had told him not to put any metal in his mouth, High Backed Wolf had held a bullet between his teeth while reloading his pistol.)

71

Crazy Horse tried to recover his friend's body but he couldn't get near it. Instead, he had to lead the decoy party in a shamefaced retreat back across the river, knowing that High Backed Wolf was dead because they had failed to obey orders.

At dawn the next morning, Crazy Horse and High Backed Wolf's grieving father stole across the river and retrieved the body. That afternoon, Crazy Horse and his decoys again rode down to the bridge, but no matter what they did, they couldn't lure the soldiers out. Suddenly a detail of cavalry appeared and trotted across the bridge headed for the Holy Road on their way to escort an inbound wagon train. The Oglalas and Cheyennes closed in on the soldiers, firing and shooting their arrows until Crazy Horse and some of the others recognized the commanding officer on the spirited gray horse. It was their friend, Lieutenant Caspar Collins.

As a shout went up not to shoot, Crazy Horse and the Oglalas opened a path to allow Collins and his men to return to the fort. But one of the soldiers had been wounded and he cried out not to be left behind. Collins turned and rode back to pick him up. At that moment, a volley of shots rang out and Collins' skittish horse bolted, taking off for the hills, straight toward the Cheyennes. Crazy Horse watched in dismay. There was nothing that he could do to save his friend.

A Cheyenne warrior described Collins' death: "I saw the officer sitting his saddle with a long arrow sticking in his forehead. His horse, a big gray, was running away with him. He passed me, and, looking back, I saw him go down among the crowd of warriors at my back. The smoke and dust hid everything." (The Cheyenne warriors captured Collins' horse but no one was ever able to ride him.)

An attack on the wagon train ended the great expedition. Three thousand warriors had spent weeks preparing for bat-

72

tle, marched for three days and ended up with only eight scalps and loot from a wagon train. Up in the north country, Sitting Bull had experienced the same trouble when his impatient Hunkpapa warriors had broken past their *akicita* guards and ruined their ambush the same way. The whites' line of communication was as secure as ever.

CHAPTER 14

After the disastrous Platte River Bridge expedition, everyone agreed that something had to be done. To count coup and win honors might be the way to fight tribal battles but as a military strategy against the might and firepower of the United States Army, it was worthless. Councils were held. Head men talked. And a decision was reached.

It was time to return to the old ways, the ways of their grandparents. Sixty years ago, before the Holy Road had been opened, the Oglala Sioux had been governed by seven older leaders known as the Big Bellies. These seven Big Bellies had appointed four outstanding young warriors known as shirt-wearers to enforce their decisions.

In the summer of 1865, the Oglalas chose seven older men to serve as their Big Bellies. These seven Big Bellies, the greatest of whom was Man-Afraid-of-His-Horses, would govern the people, direct when, where and how they should camp, move, hunt and wage war. In turn, the Big Bellies were to select four young braves to be shirt-wearers.

When the day came for the naming of the shirt-wearers, the people gathered as the brilliantly dressed chiefs of the *akicita* societies rode around the circle of tipis three times. On each pass, they singled out a young warrior to be a shirt-wearer and led him to the Big Bellies' lodge in the center of the circle. As each shirt-wearer was chosen, the women made the trilling sound and cried out his name, Young-Man-Afraid-of-His-Horses . . . Sword . . . American Horse. On their fourth and last sweep, the warriors rode past the lines of hopeful young men and tapped Crazy Horse, who stood quietly behind the others.

The choice of Crazy Horse was a surprise to everyone . . . including Crazy Horse. Both he and the people assumed that the Big Bellies would select the son of a prominent leader for the fourth shirt-wearer, just as they had for the first three. Why, Crazy Horse was the son of Worm, a modest holy man. It was true that Crazy Horse may not have been from a prominent family but he had no equal as a warrior. Even more important, the Big Bellies knew that his main concern had always been the well-being of his people.

With everyone following, the warriors escorted Crazy Horse to the large central lodge. Hardly able to believe the honor that had been laid on his shoulders, Crazy Horse seated himself with the other three shirt-wearers across from the Big Bellies. A great feast was served by the women, kettles of soup, hump rib roasts, bowls of mushrooms and cane shoots and turnips, wild fruits, and because it was a special event, boiled young dog.

After everyone had finished eating, the elders of the tribe were asked to stand and instruct the shirt-wearers in their solemn duties. You must enforce the Big Bellies' commands, Crazy Horse, Young-Man-Afraid-of-His-Horses, Sword and

American Horse were told. You must lead the warriors both in camp and on the march, keep order, prevent violence, see to it that all the people have their rights respected and no person imposes his will on another. Because the welfare of the people must always come first, you are to think not of yourselves but of others, especially widows, orphans and those with no power. And you are to carry out your responsibilities cheerfully and with strong hearts. Using an old Sioux expression, the elders advised the shirt-wearers to ignore any word spoken against them, just as they would ignore a dog lifting his leg at their tipi.

The four shirt-wearers were then presented with their shirts. Sewn of bighorn sheepskins, the shirts were decorated with beautiful quillwork and painted either blue and yellow or red and green: blue for the Sky, yellow for the Rock, red for the Sun and green for the Earth. The sleeves were fringed with locks of hair representing the people the shirt-wearers were to protect, as well as the coups that they had counted. Two hundred and forty hairlocks hung from Crazy Horse's quilled sleeves.

Three of the shirt-wearers accepted the honor with pride as their due. Only one, Crazy Horse, lowered his eyes as if he were not worthy. He had never sought attention and now the eyes of all the people were on him, including the eyes of Black Buffalo Woman, who stood in the crowd with one son beside her and an infant son on her back. Crazy Horse still loved Black Buffalo Woman but now that he had taken a vow to watch over all the people, he knew that he would have to put his feelings for her aside.

Only a month later, Crazy Horse witnessed his old friends, He Dog and Big Road, become shirt-wearers, too. The time for testing for the shirt-wearers, and all the Oglalas, was fast approaching. Gold, the metal that drove the whites to madness, had been discovered in the Montana Territory and the trail that led to the gold fields cut through the Powder River country.

CHAPTER 15

In 1862, a trapper named John Bozeman had blazed a trail that began near Fort Laramie and ran through the Sioux' Powder River hunting grounds to the newly discovered gold fields in the Montana Territory. Within three years, the angry Sioux hostiles had made travel on what became known as the Bozeman Trail so hazardous that the Army had to be called in to keep the road open.

In the Moon of the Ripe Plums, August, 1865, three columns of cavalrymen under General P. E. Connor started off into the Powder River country with orders to "attack and kill every male Indian over twelve years of age." One column bumbled and marched around for two months without so much as seeing a hostile. The other two columns either found hostiles, or the hostiles found them. Although Connor's column attacked a Cheyenne village and a friendly Arapaho village, there were few other skirmishes. The soldiers, who had already served in the Civil War, had little taste for more fighting. Caught in unseasonably cold weather, they were frequently lost and constantly harassed by war parties, many of which were led by Crazy Horse. About all the soldiers were able to accomplish was the building of a post 169 miles north of Fort Laramie called Camp Connor.

Staggering back to Fort Laramie in the Moon of the Yellow Leaves, September, the soldiers, who had been forced to slaughter their pack mules for food, were in a state of starvation and total exhaustion. The hostiles, on the other hand, did very well by what was called the Great Powder River Expedition. They had taken scalps, counted coup and stolen American horses, mules, food, supplies and guns.

If fighting the hostiles didn't succeed, the United States government reasoned, then maybe bribery would. In the spring of 1866, peace commissioners arrived at Fort Laramie with gifts and promises of money if the hostiles would sign a treaty which would keep the Bozeman Trail open to all travel. Although plenty of friendlies signed and, in return, received handsome gifts, including guns and ammunition, not one hostile touched the pen. (Because the Sioux had no written language, a head man would put his hand on the pen, while one of the whites signed.)

Although Crazy Horse and the other hard-core hostiles would have nothing to do with the peace commission, Chief Red Cloud and the Big Belly, Man-Afraid-of-His-Horses, were willing to parley, especially if it meant acquiring guns and ammunition. But after the two chiefs arrived at Fort Laramie, a Brulé chief learned from Colonel Henry Carrington, whom the Sioux called Little White Chief, that the Army had already begun to build forts along the Bozeman Trail.

When Red Cloud heard this, he was enraged. "The Great Father sends us presents and wants us to sell him the road, but

White Chief goes with soldiers to steal the road before Indians say Yes or No,'' he stormed as he and his party stalked out of the council tent. The Brulés felt differently. Spotted Tail, who had come to Fort Laramie with his dying daughter, touched the pen to the treaty, along with a number of other Brulé leaders.

Signatures or no signatures, by the end of the summer of 1866, the Army had a string of forts in the Powder River country. Camp Connor had been overhauled and renamed Fort Reno. Fort Phil Kearny had been constructed sixty-seven miles northwest of Fort Reno high on a plateau at the foot of the Bighorn Mountains. Fort C. F. Smith was being constructed ninety-one miles northwest of Fort Phil Kearny in the Montana Territory. Red Cloud, who had become the military leader of the Oglalas, and Crazy Horse, who was his second in command, were quick to realize that if they failed to drive the whites out of the Powder River country, their last buffalo hunting grounds would be lost. Without the buffalo, the Sioux were doomed.

At least one thousand Oglalas, Miniconjous, some Sans Arcs, Brulés and Hunkpapas, as well as Northern Cheyennes and Northern Arapahoes, who also realized that the lives of their people were at stake, set up their lodges on the Powder River, not far from Fort Phil Kearny. From there, Crazy Horse, along with Little Big Man, Hump, Lone Bear, Young-Man-Afraid-of-His-Horses and others, raided the Bozeman Trail from the Moon of the Birth of Calves, April, to the Moon of Frost in the Tipi, December, 1866, striking wagon trains, Army supply wagons, gold prospectors and anyone else who set foot on the Bozeman Trail. Gradually, all traffic ground to a halt.

The hostiles may have closed the Bozeman Trail to travel

but the three Powder River forts were still manned and fortified. Although Red Cloud constantly led war parties in raids against Fort Phil Kearny, he knew that despite the hostiles' greater numbers, they had too few guns to attack the fort directly. Their best chance was to target the fort's one weak link, its need for wood for fuel and ongoing construction. With the nearest stand of pines some five miles from the fort, Crazy Horse often joined Red Cloud on a nearby ridge coordinating strikes against the woodcutting parties with signals flashed from the hand mirror he wore around his neck.

In the Moon of Frost in the Tipi, December, 1866, Red Cloud, who at forty-four was no longer an active warrior, made plans to launch an attack on Fort Phil Kearny. A decoy party would lure the soldiers out of the fort into the open where the warriors, who now numbered two thousand men, could overpower them. But when they tried to carry out the ambush, it was the same old story. The decoy party turned to fight instead of leading the soldiers to the main body of waiting warriors. With only minor losses, the soldiers quickly retreated to the safety of their fort.

Crazy Horse, who had been watching, was furious. He had learned his lesson at the Platte River Bridge. Now these warriors would have to learn their lesson, too. Because he knew that he wasn't a forceful speaker, he asked Hump to discipline the decoy party and make them understand that unless they obeyed orders, the battle would be lost.

A second attack was planned for December 21. The night before, a *winkte* was called in to predict how many soldiers they would be facing in the next day's battle. With a black cloth over his head, the *winkte* rode his sorrel pony over a hill in a zigzag pattern, blowing on his eagle-bone whistle. When he returned, he told Red Cloud and Crazy Horse what he had seen. "I have ten men, five in each hand; do you want them?"

"No, we do not wish them," came the answer. "Look at all these people here. Do you think that ten men are enough to go around?"

The *winkte* rode out three more times, returning the second time with twenty enemy soldiers and the third time with fifty. It wasn't until after his fourth ride that he leapt off his pony and with a shout, struck both hands on the ground. "Answer me quickly. I have a hundred or more."

Crazy Horse and the others shouted their approval. On the morrow they would kill one hundred soldiers.

The soldiers, meanwhile, were also discussing numbers. Ever since his arrival at Fort Phil Kearny, cocky Captain William Fetterman had boasted that with eighty men, he could ride through the entire Sioux nation.

On the very cold, clear morning of December 21, 1866, the woodcutters left the fort as usual. As soon as they reached the pine woods, a small war party swooped down on them. Alerted to the attack, Fetterman and exactly eighty men marched out of the fort to escort the woodcutters back to safety. Under no circumstances whatsoever, Little White Chief Carrington told Fetterman, was he to pursue the warriors over Lodge Trail Ridge.

This time Crazy Horse led a decoy party that he knew he could depend on, four shirt-wearers, He Dog, Young-Man-Afraid-of-His-Horses, American Horse and himself, as well as two Cheyennes and two Arapahoes. While the main war party remained hidden behind Lodge Trail Ridge, the decoys swung into action as soon as Fetterman and his men headed for the woods. Because of the bitter cold, Crazy Horse wore a red blanket belted around his waist, blanket leggings and high-topped buffalo moccasins instead of his usual breechcloth and moccasins.

82

At the appearance of the decoy party, a field artillery piece was fired from the fort. Immediately, Crazy Horse and the other decoys whooped and yelled and rode every which way in a show of terror. At the same time, Red Cloud signaled the small war party that was attacking the woodcutters to retreat. The unexpected activity from both directions confused Fetterman, especially when Crazy Horse galloped toward him and his eighty men, shouting and waving his blanket as if he were guarding the retreat of his comrades. It was too tempting for Fetterman, and against all orders, he commanded his men to follow the decoy party as it headed toward Lodge Trail Ridge.

With that, Crazy Horse put on the performance of his lifetime. Bringing up the rear, he beat his pony to speed him up with one hand, while actually holding him back with the other. Staying just out of firing range, he leapt off his mount twice, once pretending to tie his war rope closer and once to lift his pony's leg to check for an injury. He even led his pony on foot, running awkwardly. Finally, he sat down in disgust and built a fire in a show of giving up.

Fetterman fell for every one of Crazy Horse's stunts. He and his men pursued the decoy party the whole five miles to Lodge Trail Ridge. The ambush had worked. Crazy Horse and his decoy party had played their part faultlessly. And Hump's tongue-lashing had helped too. The warriors, who pinched their ponies' noses so that they couldn't whinny and give their position away, had remained hidden. Fetterman and his men were out of sight of the fort.

At Crazy Horse's signal to attack, the two thousand Sioux, Cheyennes and Arapahoes let it all out. Their ponies' sharp little hoofs clattered over the frozen ground as they charged, sounding their war cries, blowing their eagle-bone whistles and chanting their war songs. The Cheyenne warrior White

Elk was seventeen at the time. "For a little while Indians and soldiers were mixed up together in hand-to-hand fighting . . . the infantry were all killed," he recalled. The war party then took on the cavalry. "Here they killed every one," White Elk reported. "After all were dead, a dog was seen running away, barking, and someone called out: 'All are dead but the dog; let him carry the news to the fort,' but someone else cried out: 'No, do not let even a dog get away'; and a young man shot at it with his arrow and killed it."

In less than an hour the battle was all over. Fetterman and his eighty men lay dead. When the war party realized that they had just defeated the Army in their first major victory, their years of anger and frustration boiled over into a rampage of stripping the soldiers of their clothes and possessions, lifting scalps and mutilating the bodies. (The Sioux mutilated their enemies' bodies because they believed that the dead entered the next world in the same form that they left the old one.) Although there weren't quite the one hundred soldiers that the *winkte* had promised, the Sioux called the battle One Hundred in the Hands.

As soon as the fighting was over, Crazy Horse left the bloody scene. He and Hump had to look for Lone Bear, the friend of their childhood, the unlucky one, who had been wounded in almost every battle that he had ever fought. They found him behind a rock, unable to move, the blood from his wound already frozen. It was later said that Lone Bear "died in the arms of Crazy Horse while Hump stood by, weeping." Crazy Horse had led his warriors to victory . . . but at a painful price.

CHAPTER 16

The North Plains winter that followed the One Hundred in the Hands fight at Fort Phil Kearny was the coldest that any of the old ones could remember. Chips, the medicine man, spent his days curing snowblindness, while the starving ponies hardly had the strength to struggle out of the heavy drifts. "The snow was deep and it was very cold," Black Elk remembered. "It was a hungry winter, for the deep snow made it hard to find the elk."

Like the other men, Crazy Horse and his brother, Little Hawk, spent much of their time hunting. Although most of the game had headed south out of the worst of the weather, one day, Crazy Horse spotted a dark mass huddled in a canyon. Elk! With knives, bows and arrows at the ready, Crazy Horse and Little Hawk crept up on snowshoes until the elk got wind of their scent. The bulls were able to get away, but the weaker cows and yearlings couldn't keep up. Between the two of them, Crazy Horse and Little Hawk slit the throats of eight elk.

That night, the two brothers built a fire in the shelter of a bluff and cooked choice morsels of elk meat. First Crazy Horse offered a piece of meat to the sky, the earth and the four directions, just as he did before every meal, and then he and Little Hawk gorged on roasted elk. Afterwards, they slept very, very well. When they returned to camp the next day with their kill, they were greeted as heroes. Fresh elk from the shirt-wearer and his brother!

As the penetrating cold continued, Red Cloud's huge camp began to break up. The Southern Oglalas and Southern Cheyennes, who weren't used to the northern Plains winters, headed south where game was more plentiful. Most of Spotted Tail's Brulés and the Fort Laramie Loafers returned to the white man's agencies to live on handouts until spring. (Some Sioux left the agencies only to hunt and pick wild fruit, while others spent spring, summer and early fall in the hostile camps hunting buffalo and fighting the Crows and Shoshonis.)

After what the Army was calling the Fetterman Massacre at Fort Phil Kearny, all the military cared about was crushing the Powder River hostiles in battle. But after four years of a brutal Civil War, the country was sick of war and in the Moon of the Hairless Calves, November, 1866, the voters elected a peace party to Congress. The peace party believed that with kindness and charity, there would be no Plains warfare. What they didn't understand was that the Plains tribes, especially Red Cloud's Oglalas in the Powder River country and Sitting Bull's Hunkpapas in the north country, were willing to fight to the death to preserve their hunting grounds.

Despite their differences, both the military and the peace party shared the same goal of settling the whole country from coast to coast in a movement that was called Manifest Destiny. But standing in the path of Manifest Destiny were the Plains tribes who controlled millions of acres of prime land.

Although the military and the peace party both agreed that the Plains tribes should be moved onto permanent reservations, and soon, the two groups worked at cross-purposes.

Anxious for action, the Army was building another fort, Fort Fetterman, where the Bozeman Trail turned north into the Powder River country, to be used as a base for supplies and troops. And those troops were already on the move, marching around the plains engaging the hostiles in skirmishes until there was no chance of peace. On the other hand, the peace party, which wanted to win over the hostiles with bribery and gifts, wouldn't support the military with enough money or manpower to wage an all-out war.

Meanwhile, Crazy Horse avenged Lone Bear's death by continuing his raids on the Bozeman Trail. In the Moon of the Sore Eyes, February, 1867, he and Little Hawk rode south to Fort Reno where they spent the rest of the winter attacking Army supply trains and mail wagons, as well as anything else that moved along the Bozeman Trail.

When spring of 1867 came, it arrived with a thundering break-up of ice that turned the rivers into raging torrents. The ponies began to fatten up on lush new prairie grass that was blanketed in the yellows, whites, pinks, blues and purples of early-blooming wildflowers. Hundreds of thousands of cranes darkened the sky and filled the air with their strange high cries as they headed north. Because Crazy Horse felt the pull of the north, too, he and Little Hawk traveled back to Red Cloud's camp in the Moon of the Birth of Calves, April. Others were also riding north, including Spotted Tail's Brulés and young warriors from the Loafers' camp. It was time for the Sun Dance, the summer buffalo hunt and more raids on Fort Phil Kearny. Hay-ay, hay-ay! It promised to be a fine summer.

As soon as the weather warmed up, Crazy Horse once

again led war parties in strikes against Fort Phil Kearny. Because the soldiers had become far more cautious and couldn't be tempted out, there were no real encounters. Impatient for a good fight, some six hundred Cheyennes headed north to attack Fort C. F. Smith, while even Crazy Horse took time off to stage raids against the Crows. By the Moon of the Ripe Plums, August, Red Cloud knew that if he didn't make an all-out move against Fort Phil Kearny soon, his whole force would drift away.

But the situation at Fort Phil Kearny had changed. The new commander had constructed a little garrison near the wood-cutters' stand of pine trees some five miles west of the fort. The boxes had been taken off fourteen wagons and set end-to-end in a circle. Soldiers were posted inside the wagon-box corral, with the horses and mules being brought in at night for safekeeping. The woodcutters' camp, guarded by thirteen soldiers, was about a mile away.

Because the wagon-box corral was too well protected to attack, it was decided that Crazy Horse and Hump would lead a strike against the woodcutters' camp. When the soldiers from the wagon-box corral rushed to the aid of the woodcutters, Red Cloud's one thousand warriors would charge out of hiding and kill them all, just as they had wiped out Fetterman and his men the year before. The Oglalas were so sure of victory that they even brought along their women and children to help carry back the booty.

When Crazy Horse, Hump, Little Big Man and others stormed the woodcutters' camp early on August 2, 1867, a shot was fired at Crazy Horse. At the sound of gunfire, the eager warriors, who had been waiting months to wage war, broke rank and galloped out of the hills. The ambush was ruined.

Once the element of surprise was gone, the angry Crazy Horse had no choice but to lead his eight hundred warriors in an attack on the woodcutters' camp, while the other two hundred warriors stampeded the horse and mule herds. Although they killed four woodcutters (Crazy Horse and Little Hawk each killed one), the other woodcutters escaped into the hills. Dismounting, the warriors began to plunder and burn the tents and scalp the bodies. Furious, Crazy Horse shouted at them, slapped one or two who were sitting by the cook tent eating molasses and ordered them back on their ponies. There was no time to lose, not when the wagon-box corral was their main target.

Leading the charge, Crazy Horse had his warriors fire their arrows from under the necks of their ponies as they surrounded the wagon-box corral at a gallop. The strategy was to keep circling until the soldiers ran out of ammunition and then attack. But to Crazy Horse's amazement, the thirty-two soldiers inside the corral not only never ran out of ammunition, their guns never seemed to need reloading either. The rain of bullets just kept coming. "We thought it was some new medicine of great power that they had, for they shot so fast that it was like tearing a blanket," the Oglala Fire Thunder observed.

What Crazy Horse and the others didn't know was that instead of using muzzle-loaders that had to be loaded with powder and a bullet and then tamped down, the soldiers were using long-range breech-loading rifles. All they had to do was place the cartridge in the rear of the rifle and pull the trigger.

After five or six ponies were killed, Crazy Horse decided to change his tactics. "We left our horses in a gulch and charged on foot," Fire Thunder recalled, "but it was like

89

green grass withering in a fire. So we picked up our wounded and went away."

With six warriors killed and six more wounded, Crazy Horse had learned a bitter lesson from the three-hour battle that the Sioux called the Bad Medicine Fight of the White Man, and the whites called the Wagon Box Fight. No matter how many warriors he had, he would never again lead an attack with bows and arrows, war clubs and only a few guns against men in a fortification armed with these new, deadly, fast-shooting guns.

CHAPTER 17

Crazy Horse and his war party didn't destroy Fort Phil Kearny as they had planned. And the Army beat back the Northern Cheyennes at Fort C. F. Smith in the Hayfield Fight of August 1, 1867. Nevertheless, the military had come to realize that the Oglalas and Northern Cheyennes were too many and too powerful to defeat in open warfare. Besides, the Army needed every available soldier to guard the workers building railroads through Kansas and Nebraska.

In the spring of 1868, peace commissioners arrived at Fort Laramie with yet another peace treaty, just as they had for the past three years. But this treaty was different. The Army agreed to abandon the three forts along what had come to be known as the Bloody Bozeman. All of what is now South Dakota west of the Missouri River, including the Black Hills, would be Sioux reservation land, while the Sioux would have the right to hunt in the Powder River country ''as long as buffalo may range thereon in such numbers as to justify the chase." Called "unceded Indian territory," the Powder River hunting grounds covered the country west of the Black Hills to the summit of the Bighorn Mountains, and north from the North Platte River. (No northern boundary was mentioned.) Whites would not be allowed to enter either the Great Sioux Reservation or the "unceded Indian territory" without permission.

On the other hand, by terms of the treaty, the Sioux would no longer oppose completion of the Union Pacific Railroad that was being built across Nebraska. The treaty also stated that when the buffalo were gone, the Sioux would live in houses, farm the land and educate their children in American-run schools. (In the years to come, the Sioux would argue that the treaty had never been explained to them.)

Although the peace commissioners assumed that the Sioux would be eager to sign the treaty, Red Cloud refused even to discuss the terms until the three Bozeman Trail forts were abandoned. Finally, on July 29, 1868, the troops marched out of Fort C. F. Smith. At dawn the next morning, Crazy Horse and his companions set fire to the fort. Within a week, both Fort Phil Kearny and Fort Reno were abandoned, too . . . and torched.

Even so, Red Cloud didn't arrive at Fort Laramie until the Moon of the Hairless Calves, November, after he had made his winter meat. Proud to the end, before he touched the pen to the treaty, he "washed his hands with the dust of the floor." Afterwards, he gave a speech. He couldn't promise that defiant young warriors like Crazy Horse wouldn't continue to fight, he said, but he, Red Cloud, would never fight against the whites again. And he never did.

What was known as Red Cloud's War was over. Crazy Horse must have felt a great sense of accomplishment and

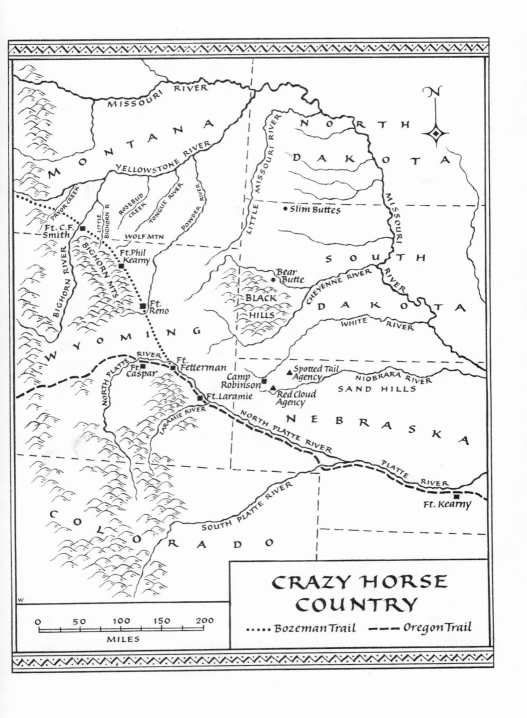

CRAZY HORSE
COUNTRY

..... Bozeman Trail   ---- Oregon Trail

MILES

0   50   100   150   200

MISSOURI RIVER

MONTANA

YELLOWSTONE RIVER

PRYOR CREEK

Ft. C.F.
Smith

LITTLE BIGHORN R

BIGHORN RIVER

ROSEBUD CREEK

TONGUE RIVER

POWDER RIVER

WOLF MTN

BIGHORN MTS

Ft. Phil
Kearny

Ft.
Reno

WYOMING

NORTH PLATTE RIVER

Ft.
Caspar

Ft.
Fetterman

Camp
Robinson

Ft. Laramie

Red Cloud
Agency

Spotted Tail
Agency

LARAMIE RIVER

NORTH PLATTE RIVER

SOUTH PLATTE RIVER

COLORADO

NORTH

DAKOTA

LITTLE MISSOURI RIVER

• Slim Buttes

SOUTH

DAKOTA

MISSOURI RIVER

Bear
Butte

BLACK
HILLS

CHEYENNE RIVER

WHITE RIVER

NEBRASKA

NIOBRARA RIVER

SAND HILLS

PLATTE RIVER

Ft. Kearny

N

W

pride. First he had been at the forefront of driving the Crows out of the Powder River country, and then he had been at the forefront of driving out the whites. Now he was free to live as he always had, in the vast land that was as abundant in wild game as any place on earth.

Unlike Red Cloud, who was given his own agency in exchange for traveling to Washington to meet the Great White Father, the President, Crazy Horse never considered coming in. But others did. While Crazy Horse hunted and led raids against the Crows and Shoshonis, wagonfuls of gifts tempted half the Powder River hostiles, some five thousand Oglalas, to come into the new Red Cloud Agency. (Spotted Tail already had his own agency south of the Black Hills.)

The following summer, in 1869, shirt-wearer Crazy Horse, with his friend, He Dog, received yet another honor. They were appointed lance bearers in a special ceremony. Wrapped in otter fur and decorated with scalps and feathers, the nine-foot-long sacred lances had been with the Oglalas even before they had crossed the Missouri River to live on the Great Plains. As long as the lances were carried into battle by brave warriors, the Oglalas believed that times would be good for them. He Dog explained: "The spears were each three or four hundred years old and were given by the older genera-tion to those in the younger generation who had best lived the life of a warrior."

Soon after the ceremony, Crazy Horse and He Dog carried the sacred lances in a raid against the Crows far to the west. Although the war party, under He Dog, was able to steal the Crows' ponies, the Crows immediately gave chase in what turned out to be a long-running battle. Finally, Crazy Horse rallied his men, countercharged and forced the Crows to retreat. Thirteen Crows were killed in the celebrated Oglala

94

victory that became known as "When They Chased the Crows Back to Camp."

Crazy Horse didn't spend all of his time hunting and warring. He often visited Black Buffalo Woman's camp where he and Black Buffalo Woman talked quietly or he simply watched her play with her young children. He even gave Black Buffalo Woman dozens of elk teeth from the hunt to decorate her fine deerskin dress.

Gossip was a favorite Sioux pastime and the village gossip was that Crazy Horse still loved Black Buffalo Woman. And if Black Buffalo Woman didn't love Crazy Horse, she certainly didn't send him on his way either. No Water should give Black Buffalo Woman her freedom so that she could marry Crazy Horse, it was agreed. But No Water was a jealous man who would never accept a few gift ponies in exchange for his wife as any self-respecting warrior was expected to do.

As a shirt-wearer and a lance bearer, Crazy Horse had vowed to think always of his people first. But early in the summer of 1870, he and Black Buffalo Woman were once again camped near each other. Crazy Horse and his people had followed the buffalo north to the Yellowstone River where they had met up with Sitting Bull and his Hunkpapas. Black Buffalo Woman, No Water and their three children, who were living at the Red Cloud Agency at the time, had also traveled north to the Yellowstone River for some hunting.

When Crazy Horse and Black Buffalo Woman saw each other again, they knew that their love was as strong as ever. They could no longer deny that they were meant to be husband and wife and they made plans to run away. The night before they eloped, Black Buffalo Woman arranged for relatives to take care of her children, while Crazy Horse put together a small war party under the pretense of going against the Crows.

The next day, Crazy Horse and Black Buffalo Woman rode off with their war party in the full light of day. Crazy Horse, who wore plain dress and whose face was unpainted as usual, had brushed and braided Black Buffalo Woman's hair and painted both the part in her hair and her face with bright vermilion just as many Sioux husbands did. Black Buffalo Woman rode straight and tall with no shame. As an Oglala woman it was her right to leave her husband and marry another.

When No Water returned from a hunting trip and found Black Buffalo Woman gone, he knew right away what had happened. Instead of releasing his wife, No Water, in a fury, borrowed a revolver and rounded up his comrades to track down the two lovers.

On their second day out, Crazy Horse and Black Buffalo Woman stopped at Little Big Man's camp and it was there that No Water found them. After racing frantically from tipi to tipi, No Water finally yanked back the door flap of the tipi where Crazy Horse and Black Buffalo Woman were sitting by the fire with their friends. No Water waved his pistol.

"My friend, I have come!" he shouted.

Crazy Horse leapt to his feet and reached for his knife but Little Big Man, in an attempt to avoid violence, held back his arm, just as Crazy Horse's vision had foreseen. No Water fired. The bullet struck Crazy Horse below his nose and shattered his upper jaw. As he fell into the fire, Black Buffalo Woman screamed and fled out the back of the tipi. Before anyone could stop him, No Water ran out, shouted to his comrades that he had killed Crazy Horse, jumped on the nearest pony and rode away.

Although Crazy Horse wasn't dead, he was gravely wounded. "Let go! Let go of my arm!" he cried out over and over, doubtless reliving his vision. Because he was unable to speak clearly, as he slowly recovered, he indicated by sign language that Black Buffalo Woman was not to be blamed and that there must be no more trouble. Crazy Horse's friends clamored for revenge but No Water gave Crazy Horse's father, Worm, three of his finest ponies. By accepting the gift, Worm indicated that the matter was closed. Luckily, Crazy Horse's hot-tempered brother, Little Hawk, was off on a raid or there might have been open warfare.

The situation was bad enough as it was. No Water was guilty of trying to murder Crazy Horse, as well as not allowing Black Buffalo Woman to leave him. Crazy Horse, on the other hand, was guilty of breaking his shirt-wearer vows by putting his own happiness above the well-being of his people.

The old ones immediately set to work keeping the peace. With a great exchange of ponies, a measure of calm returned to the camps as they arranged for Black Buffalo Woman to go back to her husband. Fellow shirt-wearer He Dog later commented: "When we were made chiefs, we were bound by very strict rules as to what we should do and what not to do, which were very hard for us to follow . . . I have always kept the oaths I made then, but Crazy Horse did not."

No longer allowed to be a shirt-wearer, Crazy Horse took his bighorn sheepskin shirt from its case and, with heavy heart, returned it. But the Big Bellies couldn't agree on who should take his place. The arguing went on for so long that the whole system finally ground to a halt and the Big Bellies never met again. He Dog lamented: "The shirt was never given to anyone else. Everything seemed to stop right there. Everything began to fall to pieces."

By putting his personal feelings above all else, Crazy Horse had shattered the Oglalas' first steps at organizing a central governing body. In their struggle to hold onto their land in the years to come, that lack of a central authority would always work against them. And Crazy Horse's good name was ruined. During his twenties, he had risen high in the Sioux world. Now, as he neared his thirties, he had lost everything. More important, he had hurt those whom he cared about most deeply, his people.

CHAPTER 18

Although Crazy Horse was still recovering from his gunshot wound, he decided to meet up with his brother. He had just arrived at Little Hawk's camp along the Yellowstone River when two members of Little Hawk's war party that had gone out against the Shoshonis rode in. Their faces were streaked with dirt and their blankets torn. They were in mourning. A band of white miners who called themselves the Big Horners had ambushed their war party, they said. While the others had fled, Little Hawk had stayed behind to charge the whites alone. He had been killed with a single shot in the back.

Little Hawk, the bravest of them all, the risk-taker, his quick-tempered brother who held the promise of becoming one of the greatest of all Oglala warriors, was dead. Shot in the back! Bitterness rose in Crazy Horse's throat like gall. If only he, Crazy Horse, hadn't been caught up in his own lovesick schemes, he might have been in the war party and Little Hawk might still be alive.

Little Hawk . . . with Little Hawk Crazy Horse hadn't been the silent one. There were so many times that they had laughed together, teasing their older sister across the tipi fire, and teasing each other mercilessly. And when they had gone into battle, they had fought as one. How like Little Hawk to die bringing up the rear to protect the others.

Crazy Horse went buffalo hunting the next day to try and ease his pain. As he neared camp with the fat buffalo cow he had killed and butchered, he thought that he saw Moccasin Top and another man in the distance. The second man jumped on Moccasin Top's pony and rode away.

"Are you still here?" Crazy Horse asked as he approached Moccasin Top. "Then who was the man that just rode off on your buckskin?"

"That was No Water," came the reply.

"I wish I had known it!" Crazy Horse cried. "I would certainly have given him a bullet in return for the one he gave me."

Although Crazy Horse set out in pursuit, No Water escaped across the Yellowstone River. Soon after, he returned to the Red Cloud Agency with Black Buffalo Woman and their three children. Some time later, word came back to the Oglalas that a light-haired, light-complexioned daughter had been born to Black Buffalo Woman. "They claim that a few months after she went back to No Water, this woman gave birth to a light-haired little girl," He Dog recalled. "Many people believe this child was Crazy Horse's daughter, but it was never known for certain." And if Crazy Horse knew, he never said.

It was time that Crazy Horse was married, his friends He Dog and Red Feather agreed. He had suffered too many losses and needed the warmth of his own tipi fire and a wife to care for him.

100

One summer day Crazy Horse returned to his family tipi to find Black Shawl tending the fire. Black Shawl was a quiet one, like Crazy Horse, and older than most unmarried Oglala women, nearing thirty. Black Shawl's brother, Red Feather, said later, "Both Crazy Horse and my sister stayed single much longer than is usual among our people."

The two were suited to each other and Crazy Horse's life again began to take on meaning as he and Black Shawl moved into their own tipi. Now he sat in the place of honor, well looked after, with the fragrance of sweet-grass and cherry bark laid on the hot coals to let all the village know that their marriage was a good one. As was the Sioux practice, an old woman relative of Black Shawl's came to live with them, which meant that Crazy Horse had the choice piece of meat in his soup, extra moccasins to take on war parties and the parfleches for winter eating always filled.

Crazy Horse was comforted, too, by having Black Shawl ride beside him as he made the sad journey into Shoshoni country to recover Little Hawk's remains. Dusty and tired, they came back a month later after having wrapped Little Hawk's bones in a red blanket and laid the bundle on a death scaffold in a place safe from the enemy.

Soon after their return, in the Moon of the Falling Leaves, October, 1870, Crazy Horse and Hump, along with He Dog and Red Feather, got up a small war party to go against the Shoshonis. But the weather turned cold and a wet snow began to fall. Although Crazy Horse tried to call off the raid against what turned out to be a much larger force, Hump complained.

"The last time you called off a fight here, when we got back to camp they laughed at us," Hump told Crazy Horse. "You and I have our good name to think about."

"You have a good gun and I have a good gun, but look at

our men!'' Crazy Horse replied. ''None of them have good guns and most of them have only bows and arrows. It's a bad place for a fight and a bad day for it, and the enemy are twelve to our one.''

But because Hump insisted, they fought. Badly outnumbered, Crazy Horse called a retreat, with Hump, Good Weasel and himself bringing up the rear. Crazy Horse attacked the pursuing Shoshonis from one side, while Hump and Good Weasel attacked from the other. When they came together, Hump's pony was limping.

''We're up against it now; my horse has a wound in the leg,'' Hump said.

''I know it,'' Crazy Horse agreed. ''We were up against it from the start.''

Nevertheless, the three warriors charged the Shoshonis again. This time Hump's pony didn't make it. As Hump went down, the Shoshonis surged over him. In the slush and snow, and hopelessly outnumbered, there was nothing that Crazy Horse could do. He never saw his *kola,* his best friend, Hump, again.

''Four days later Crazy Horse and I went back to find High Back Bone [Hump] and bury him,'' Red Feather later said. ''We didn't find anything but the skull and a few bones. High Back Bone had been eaten by coyotes already. There weren't any Shoshonis around. When the Shoshonis found out whom they had killed, they beat it.''

Crazy Horse was devastated. First Lone Bear, then Little Hawk and now Hump. With the death of his only brother and his two oldest friends, the carefree days of Crazy Horse's youth faded into a pale memory.

CHAPTER 19

Within a year of their marriage, Black Shawl gave birth to a baby girl. She apologized to her husband for not having given him a son but Crazy Horse wouldn't hear of it. Announcing that his daughter would grow up to be such a great mother of her people that everyone would stand in awe of her sacred ways, he named her They-Are-Afraid-of-Her. Crazy Horse doted on the child, tickling her with a rabbit's tail to make her giggle and playing with her by the hour.

Although Crazy Horse still smoked the short pipe of one who was no longer in high standing, with the birth of his daughter, both the scar on his face and the scars in his heart began to heal. Gradually, he began to reach out to others.

Gathering up the young boys of the village, Crazy Horse taught them everything that he had learned as a boy. He showed them how to make bows and arrows, how to track game, hunt, fight, read weather patterns, survive on the prairie and heal wounds. He taught them to know the nature of animals, birds and plants. He explained how Wakan Tanka, the Great Spirit, was the maker of all things of earth, sky and water. And he told them tales of their Sioux heritage that had been handed down from generation to generation.

Unknowingly, Crazy Horse began to attain that highest of the four virtues. He had always been brave and everyone knew that he had the fortitude to endure suffering. He had been unfailingly generous since he was a child and had even given away Little Hawk's pony herd instead of keeping it for himself as was the custom. Now, as he gained insight into his Oglala heritage and the life of his people, he gave away more than just possessions. He gave of himself in order to inspire others, the beginning of that greatest of virtues, wisdom.

Crazy Horse may still not have earned back the full respect of his people but he never lost the respect of his enemies. A Crow captive later told how his warriors "knew Crazy Horse had a medicine-gun that never missed, and that he was bullet-proof."

Respect for Crazy Horse spread north, too, to the Yellowstone River country of Sitting Bull and his Hunkpapa Sioux. Although Crazy Horse was some ten years younger than Sitting Bull, their single-minded resistance to the white threat drew them together and they became strong allies and friends.

In 1868, when Sitting Bull had been chosen chief of all the Northern Sioux, Northern Cheyennes and Northern Arapahoes, Crazy Horse had been made his second in command. From now on, they agreed, they would fight the whites only when the whites attacked or invaded Sioux land in an if-they-come-shooting-we'll-shoot-back pact.

Although Crazy Horse and Sitting Bull were both celebrated warriors, they were very different. Sitting Bull was an

104

outspoken leader, holy man, speech-maker, composer, singer of songs, teacher, philosopher and medicine man. The modest Crazy Horse was just the opposite. "He never spoke in council and attended very few," He Dog said. "There was no special reason for this; it was just his nature. He was a very quiet man except when there was fighting."

Despite their differences, or maybe because of them, the two warriors competed for honors. Their day of testing came in the Moon of the Ripe Plums, August, 1872, when a survey party, escorted by nearly five hundred soldiers, marched into their Yellowstone River country to survey for the Northern Pacific Railroad. Although the 1868 Fort Laramie Treaty hadn't set a northern boundary to the "unceded Indian territory," the hostiles considered the Yellowstone River country to be theirs. As soon as they learned that whites were camped on the Yellowstone River opposite the mouth of Arrow Creek (now Pryor Creek), they prepared for war.

On August 14, 1872, Crazy Horse and Sitting Bull led an expedition of Oglalas, Hunkpapas, Sans Arcs, Miniconjous and Blackfeet-Sioux against the surveyors and their military escort. But many of the northern Sioux had never fought white forces before. When they saw the soldiers' big American horses and herds of cattle, they rode out of hiding with great shouts and war cries to stampede and capture the animals.

With the surprise of the ambush spoiled, the two sides formed lines and began to exchange long-range firing. After a couple of hours, Crazy Horse decided that it was time to make a move. Not only did he want to draw the soldiers into open warfare, but he also wanted to give these Hunkpapa cousins a demonstration of Oglala bravery. Staying just out of range, Crazy Horse rode his pony very, very slowly between the Sioux and Army forces along what was called the "daring line." Although bullets cropped his pony's tail and splintered his lance, Crazy Horse was unharmed. The watching warriors cheered his courage.

That was too much for Sitting Bull. As soon as Crazy Horse returned to the Sioux lines, Sitting Bull made *his* move. Taking his long-stemmed pipe and pouch of tobacco, Sitting Bull walked out between the two lines. With bullets flying all around him, he sat down, filled his pipe with tobacco and lit it. Pointing first to the sky, the earth and the four directions, he then began to smoke as calmly as if he were seated in his own tipi. After he had smoked the pipe down, Sitting Bull carefully cleaned it, returned it to its pouch and strolled back to his lines. No warrior, or soldier, either, who saw Sitting Bull's bravery that day ever forgot it.

But Crazy Horse wasn't about to admit that he had been bested. "Let's make one more circle toward the soldier line," he called to a comrade. With all the soldiers firing at them, the two warriors rode out. After a display of horsemanship, they turned to head back. But a shot felled Crazy Horse's pony. Leaping to his feet, he ran the rest of the way on foot.

Although the Battle of Arrow Creek was pretty much of a draw, there was no question that Sitting Bull had won the war honors for the day. But Crazy Horse had won something, too, the renewed respect of the Oglalas. "Later on the older, more responsible men of the tribe conferred another kind of chieftainship on Crazy Horse," He Dog reported. "He was made war chief of the whole Oglala tribe."

CHAPTER 20

When the surveyors and their Army escort headed back to the Missouri River not long after the Battle of Arrow Creek, Crazy Horse and Sitting Bull were convinced that their show of force had scared the whites off. Actually, the surveyors had left because their work was finished. Sure enough, the following summer they were back, this time led by a warrior whose name would be forever linked with Crazy Horse's, Lieutenant Colonel George Armstrong Custer.

In many ways, Crazy Horse and Custer were alike. About the same age, they were both ardent patriots who had made warfare the keystone of their lives. Custer had fought in the Civil War when Americans killed Americans by the thousands. Now he was fighting another war in which Americans were again killing Americans, although probably neither Crazy Horse nor Custer would have viewed the conflict that way.

By the Moon of the Ripe Plums, August, 1873, the survey

party's wagon train of fifteen hundred soldiers and four hundred civilians, escorted by Custer's 7th Cavalry, had penetrated deep into Sioux territory. Crazy Horse and Sitting Bull, with some 350 Sioux and Cheyenne warriors, followed their progress to where the Tongue River flowed into the Yellowstone.

Taking a position high on a bluff overlooking Custer's camp, Crazy Horse studied the scene below through his white man's binoculars. It was a hot and dusty August 4th and Custer's cavalrymen were loafing as they waited for the rest of the expedition to catch up. Crazy Horse counted only eighty-five soldiers but they were all well armed and he had learned from experience that his larger force couldn't make up for its lack of guns. Guns . . . warfare with the whites always seemed to come down to guns.

An ambush, like the ambush that had fooled Fetterman and his men at Fort Phil Kearny, might work. Within minutes, the quiet of the windless, sultry day was shattered. A decoy party of six Sioux burst out of hiding and galloped toward the cavalry's horses, yelling and waving their blankets to stampede the herd toward a stand of trees where the main war party was hidden. As the six Sioux rode back and forth just out of range, shouting insults and firing their guns, Custer, who had been napping, grabbed his rifle, pulled on his clothes and boots and ordered his men to mount up.

Calling for twenty men to ride with him, Custer headed out after the decoy party. But he was well aware of what had happened to Fetterman. He reined his horse up short and just as he suspected, the decoy party reined their mounts up short, too.

In that brief moment beside the deep blue Yellowstone River, the two forces took each other's measure. A horse

108

whinnied in the stillness and somewhere a bird called. Custer had certainly heard of Crazy Horse, but he probably wouldn't have singled out the slightly built warrior with only a lightning streak on his face, a few hail spots on his body and a single feather in his long hair as the great war chief, Crazy Horse. The other warriors, with their brilliant war paint and magnificent war bonnets, were far more impressive.

Custer might not have recognized Crazy Horse, but Crazy Horse surely knew who Custer was. Called Long Hair by the hostiles, Custer's shoulder-length red-gold hair gave him away. Five years before, Long Hair Custer and his 7th Cavalry had crept up on a Cheyenne village on the Washita River in the Indian Territory of Oklahoma and killed more than one hundred men, women and children, including Chief Black Kettle. (It was the same village that had been attacked at Sand Creek.)

Afterwards, a number of the Cheyenne survivors had joined Crazy Horse and Sitting Bull's war party. Now, at the sight of the hated Long Hair, there was no holding them back. They plunged out of the woods, screaming and yelping and firing their arrows. At the break in discipline, the others galloped out, too. Faced with 350 mounted braves bearing down on them, Long Hair and his cavalrymen quickly retreated.

Led by the enraged Cheyennes, Crazy Horse and his war party set out in pursuit, never suspecting that Long Hair had ordered his men to dismount and lie down in the tall grass where they couldn't be seen. As the warriors pounded toward them, the soldiers let loose with a volley of bullets that scattered the hostiles. Although Crazy Horse quickly regrouped his men out of range, he couldn't control the Cheyennes. Wild to get at Long Hair, they rode out one by one, fired off a shot or an arrow and dashed back. Having learned that such individual acts of courage were useless against the Army's guns, Crazy Horse and Sitting Bull set fire to the grass to smoke the soldiers out. But there was little wind and the flames sputtered and died.

With the advantage of a well-armed force, Long Hair ordered his men to mount up and attack. Taken by surprise, and knowing that their weapons were no match for the cavalry's carbines, Crazy Horse gave the command to withdraw and head back to camp. He and Sitting Bull never considered themselves to have been defeated. On the contrary, they believed that they had successfully challenged the enemy. The Sioux John Stands in Timber explained their reasoning. "Once warriors were satisfied that they had acquitted themselves well and gained honors, had halted the enemy and rendered him powerless, or secured their camps and enabled their women and children to get away, they saw no sense in risking further the lives of their brave men."

After returning to their village and gathering up their people, Crazy Horse and Sitting Bull led them across the Yellowstone River from the north bank to the south bank. Mounted on their strong little ponies, the men pulled the women, children and helpless ones across the river on rafts or on the skin bundles of their tipis. It was only after they had set up camp on the south bank that they realized that Long Hair had followed them.

Guided by his Crow and Arikara scouts, Long Hair had set out in pursuit to engage the hostiles in another, more decisive, battle. But what had been simple for the Sioux and Cheyennes was impossible for the 7th Cavalry. Their horses simply couldn't make it across the deep, swift Yellowstone River. Finally, after an all-day attempt to ford the river by

110

other means, Long Hair gave up and ordered his men to set up camp on the north bank. No doubt the soldiers' futile efforts to cross the river greatly amused the watching hostiles.

At dawn on August 11, 1873, a party of warriors began to fire guns and arrows across the Yellowstone River at Long Hair's camp. Black Shawl, They-Are-Afraid-of-Her and the other women and children of the village, who were eager to see Long Hair get what he deserved, climbed the bluff above the river to sing out strong-heart songs and call encouragement to their men.

While the hostiles kept up a steady barrage of gunfire and arrows from the south bank, Crazy Horse and several hundred mounted warriors forded the river to the north bank, again an easy feat. To hem in Long Hair's men, Crazy Horse had half the war party land above the soldiers' camp and the other half land below. But with most of their guns on the south side of the river, the hostiles were caught short when Long Hair gave the same mount-and-attack order that had routed Crazy Horse's war party the week before. Once again, the hostiles had to flee before the cavalry's overwhelming firepower. With Long Hair and his men in full pursuit, they rode a hard nine miles before they could recross the Yellowstone River to the safety of the south bank.

Soon after the Battle of the Yellowstone, Crazy Horse and Sitting Bull led their people up the Bighorn River where they camped for the rest of the summer. Meanwhile, Custer and his 7th Cavalry returned to their fort on the Missouri River. Both sides were well pleased with the outcome of their skirmishes. Crazy Horse and Sitting Bull were certain that they had seen the last of the soldiers, while Custer was equally sure that he had given the hostiles a lesson that they would not soon forget. As it turned out, they were both wrong.

CHAPTER 21

Early in the summer of 1874, Crazy Horse left Black Shawl and They-Are-Afraid-of-Her in camp along the Little Bighorn River to lead a small war party against the Crows. Crazy Horse was troubled. Black Shawl's buckskin dress hung loose from weight she had lost, and when the weather turned cold or damp, she coughed as if from the white man's disease of tuberculosis.

They-Are-Afraid-of-Her wasn't strong either. Her dark eyes were big in her thin face as she looked up at her father and begged, "Pony! Pony!" But when Crazy Horse swung her up on his shoulders and galloped around for the ride-the-pony game that she loved, she tired quickly. Often, when visitors arrived and stayed long talking, she would fall asleep in her father's arms.

Crazy Horse and his warriors didn't have much success against the Crows, just a few horses stolen. Although they weren't gone long, when they returned, they found that their people had packed up and moved on. At least there were signs on buffalo heads and sticks that pointed the way east toward the Tongue River. On reaching the Tongue River a few days later, Crazy Horse and his war party spotted the blue smoke of village fires rising above the bluffs. But no one came out to greet them as they usually did when a war party returned. It was only as the warriors drew nearer that they saw why. Their people wore tattered blankets and their hair, dusted with dirt, hung loose.

Crazy Horse, and every man in his war party, must have caught his breath in a moment of dread. Someone had died. As Crazy Horse led his warriors slowly through the path that the people opened for them, he saw his father, Worm, and his uncle, Little Hawk, who, after young Little Hawk's death, had taken his nephew's name. One look at their torn clothing and stricken expressions and Crazy Horse knew that it was to his lodge that death had come.

Not again! Not another death! Worm quietly took the rope of Crazy Horse's pony and the sage hens that he had shot as a treat for Black Shawl and They-Are-Afraid-of-Her. Worm took his bow, too, although Crazy Horse held on to his Winchester rifle as always.

"Son, be strong," Worm murmured as he and Little Hawk followed Crazy Horse to his lodge.

Crazy Horse pulled back the door flap. The fire was out and the lodge was dark but he could see the figure of Black Shawl swaying back and forth and hear her sorrowful keening. Her dress was torn and her face was streaked with dirt. Crazy Horse reeled as if from the blow of a war club. Death had taken his beloved daughter from him.

"Be strong, my son!" Worm urged again.

But there was no being strong. His daughter with the light

brown hair and the light complexion so much like his own was gone. Not until that night was Crazy Horse able to ask what They-Are-Afraid-of-Her had died of. The white man's disease, Worm told him, the coughing sickness.

Aagh, it wasn't enough that the white men killed with their loud, fast-shooting guns. Now they had invaded his very lodge to kill silently with disease. When he could bring himself to speak again, Crazy Horse asked where They-Are-Afraid-of-Her's death scaffold was. Knowing his son, Worm answered reluctantly. They-Are-Afraid-of-Her was a two-day journey away to the west, in Crow country. Don't go, Worm pleaded. It would be dangerous to travel there alone. But danger meant nothing to Crazy Horse, not when he hadn't even bid his daughter a final farewell.

Leaving the grieving Black Shawl to be comforted by her relatives, Crazy Horse started out. Two days later, on a beautiful summer morning, when white clouds drifted in an azure sky, he came upon the place of death that his father had described. They-Are-Afraid-of-Her's scaffold had been set on a grassy level at the edge of a few trees. And on the scaffold was a tiny, red-blanketed figure. From the scaffold's posts hung the playthings that They-Are-Afraid-of-Her had loved the most, a rattle of antelope hoofs strung on rawhide, a bounding bladder filled with pebbles, a painted willow hoop.

As Crazy Horse approached where his daughter lay, he saw that tied on top of the red blanket was They-Are-Afraid-of-Her's favorite deerskin doll. It was tucked in its doll cradleboard that was beaded with the same design that beaded They-Are-Afraid-of-Her's little buckskin dresses, a design that had been handed down from mother to daughter in Black Shawl's family for generations.

Such a tiny child needed the protection of her father. Crazy

114

Horse hadn't been with They-Are-Afraid-of-Her when she had died but he could be with her now. Climbing up on the scaffold, Crazy Horse lay down beside the little bundle. But the finality of his loss overwhelmed him and he buried his face in his arms as the scaffold shook under the weight of his grief.

For three days and three nights, Crazy Horse protected his daughter. Although buzzards circled high overhead and a wolf sniffed around the legs of the scaffold, the sight and smell of life kept them at a distance. And then, on the third day, a thick fog blew in as far-off lightning flickered and thunder rumbled. Climbing stiffly down, Crazy Horse unhobbled his pony and with a heavy heart, rode away, leaving the little red bundle behind forever.

Caspar Collins, Lone Bear, Hump, Little Hawk and now They-Are-Afraid-of-Her. Too many deaths. Too much pain. From that time on, everyone noticed that Crazy Horse fought with a new recklessness. Although his people wondered if he were courting death, He Dog later laughed at the idea that his friend Crazy Horse had ever thrown away his rifle and fought with only a war club or a pony-whip as others did who sought death.

"All the time I was in fights with Crazy Horse in critical moments of the fight, Crazy Horse would always jump off his horse to fire," He Dog said. "He wanted to be sure that he hit what he aimed at. That is the kind of fighter he was. He didn't like to start a battle unless he had it all planned out in his head and knew he was going to win. He always used judgment and played safe."

In his day-to-day living, Crazy Horse grew even quieter and more remote. He almost never spoke in public, let alone tried to stir up his people with passionate speeches the way Sitting Bull did. Instead, he consulted in private on strategy

115

with other warriors, mostly listening and talking only when he had something of importance to say.

Even though Crazy Horse's days as a shirt-wearer and lance-bearer were long behind him, he was increasingly looked up to. He didn't seek power or even seem to care about it but gradually he gathered around him a band of loyal followers who became known as the Crazy Horse People. It was only because they were as dedicated as he to safeguarding their freedom that Crazy Horse, in an attempt to make some kind of sense out of the deaths of his loved ones, was willing to act as their leader.

CHAPTER 22

Although the Sioux knew that there was gold in the Black Hills, it was a forbidden subject. Crazy Horse's father, Worm, had even attended a council where it was agreed that any person who told a white man about the gold should be killed. After all, it was greed for gold that had ruined the hunting grounds of the Platte valley as thousands of white emigrants traveled the Holy Road on their way to the California gold fields. And it was greed for gold in the Montana Territory that had cut the Bozeman Trail through the Sioux' Powder River country.

The Black Hills, which the Sioux called Paha Sapa (meaning "the hills that are black"), were at the heart of their religion. The home of Wakan Tanka, the Great Spirit, Paha Sapa was where the Sioux held sacred ceremonies and where young men went in search of a vision. Since it was a holy place, the Sioux didn't live in Paha Sapa, although they entered from time to time to cut down pine trees for their lodgepoles, harvest plants for medicine and dyes or hunt game when buffalo were scarce.

How the Sioux viewed Paha Sapa didn't matter to the American people. Rumors flew that there was gold in the Black Hills and that was that. Under orders, Colonel George A. Custer marched into the Black Hills at the head of more than one thousand men on July 25, 1874. Despite denials, the presence of miners, geologists and newspaper reporters in the wagon train made it clear that Custer's expedition was looking for gold.

Following a trail that the Sioux came to call the Thieves' Road, Custer's party was awed by the magnificent scenery. Only about sixty miles wide and 120 miles long, the Black Hills' lofty granite peaks, forests of dark ponderosa pine and rushing mountain streams were in dramatic contrast to the rolling, treeless grasslands that surrounded them. One of the reporters with Custer wrote that the Black Hills was "one of the most beautiful spots on God's green earth. No wonder the Indians regard this as the home of the Great Spirit and guard it with jealous care."

Ironically, when Custer and his men marched out of the Black Hills a few weeks later, they camped at the foot of Bear Butte, the site of Sioux gatherings. From there, Custer sent out enthusiastic accounts of the gold the expedition had found, as well as a description of the spectacular scenery. At the news, Americans began to head for the Black Hills in droves, either to look for gold or to stake out land.

But the race for the Black Hills presented the government with a problem. The 1868 Fort Laramie Treaty, which had been signed by Sioux leaders and United States peace commissioners, had been ratified by the United States Senate. It guaranteed that the Great Sioux Reservation, which included the Black Hills, would be ''set apart for the absolute and undisturbed use and occupation of the Indians . . . and the United States now solemnly agrees that no persons . . . shall ever be permitted to pass over, settle upon, or reside in the territory.''

Even though Crazy Horse and his people were camped in the Powder River country, they, like Sioux everywhere, were very much aware that their sacred land was being violated. In the late summer and fall of 1874, Crazy Horse often rode off by himself, never saying where he was going or when he would be back. To the concern of Black Shawl and his parents, Crazy Horse sometimes disappeared for weeks and when he returned, he was as silent as when he had left.

It was during that time that bodies of white miners were found here and there in Paha Sapa. An arrow was always thrust into the ground beside them, even if they had been shot with a bullet. When the Crazy Horse People heard that the bodies were never cut up, mutilated or even scalped as might have been expected, they remembered that Crazy Horse's brother, Little Hawk, had been killed by white miners. Nothing was said and no victory dance was ever held, but the Crazy Horse People sensed that Crazy Horse had found a way to ease some of his grief.

Although the Army made a half-hearted attempt to keep the whites out of the Black Hills, there was no stopping the gold rush. Because thousands of whites were already in the Black Hills by 1875, the government began pressing the Sioux to sell their Paha Sapa. Every Sioux from the Missouri River to the Bighorn Mountains had something to say about that. First of all, how could land be sold? Land, especially sacred land, didn't belong to anyone any more than the sun or the sky did. A Sioux head man, Spotted Bear, pointed out: ''Your

119

Great White Father has a big safe, and so have we. This hill is our safe.''

Many agency Sioux had seen enough of the whites and their military strength to realize that they probably couldn't hold on to Paha Sapa anyway. Therefore, they might as well get the best possible price for it. Other agency Sioux, led by Young-Man-Afraid-of-His-Horses, who had brought his people into the Red Cloud Agency to protect the helpless ones, were opposed to the sale. Even though they lived on an agency, they tried hard to maintain the old Sioux way of life. Needless to say, the hostile Sioux, under Crazy Horse and Sitting Bull, not only refused to consider selling Paha Sapa, but they were also willing to fight, and die, if necessary, to save it.

Because consent of three-quarters of all adult Sioux males was needed to change the terms of the treaty, in the Moon of the Yellow Leaves, September, 1875, yet another commission arrived at the Red Cloud Agency from Washington for a council with the Sioux. Runners were sent in every direction to bring in the hostiles, as well as those agency Sioux who had spent the summer hunting in the Powder River country and were still out.

When Young Man Afraid arrived at Crazy Horse's camp to urge him to attend the council and speak for the hostiles, Crazy Horse refused. ''One does not sell the earth upon which the people walk,'' he replied. Although Crazy Horse spoke so quietly that those seated in the lodge circle could hardly hear him, Young Man Afraid understood his meaning loud and clear. Crazy Horse and Young Man Afraid had gone their separate ways since they had been shirt-wearers, but in the Sioux way, they didn't question each other's choices. Pained as the two old friends might have been at their differences, they parted with the crossed handshake of respect.

As it turned out, the council, which was held eight miles east of the Red Cloud Agency, was not only a failure, it also came close to being a disaster. Many more Sioux showed up than the commissioners had bargained for. On September 23, 1875, in a deliberate show of fighting strength, thousands of mounted warriors, dressed and painted for war, rode down from the hills in wave after wave. They circled the council tent, sang their war-songs and fired their rifles. Suddenly, one of Crazy Horse's head men, Little Big Man, dressed in breechcloth and war bonnet, galloped through the angry warriors, a Winchester in one hand and two revolvers in his belt. He was going to kill the white men who had come to steal Sioux lands, he shouted.

Although Little Big Man was quickly overpowered by guards, the situation was explosive. And then Young Man Afraid, whom all the Sioux respected, stepped forward. Knowing what lay in store for his people if the commissioners were killed, he spoke to the frenzied warriors.

"Go to your lodges, my foolish young friends," he ordered. "Go to your lodges and do not return until your heads have cooled!"

When Crazy Horse, who was camped nearby keeping an eye on the council, heard how the white commissioners had scurried back to the safety of nearby Camp Robinson, he was well pleased. The council had failed.

So be it, the United States government said when they heard that the Sioux wouldn't even consider an offer of $400,000 a year for mineral rights to the Black Hills, or $6,000,000 for its outright sale. (The government also offered to buy the Powder River country for $50,000 a year to be paid for in cows and farm equipment!) If the Sioux refuse to sell their land, the government reasoned, then we will have

121

to find an excuse to take it. The excuse the government came up with was that the Sioux had been raiding the Crows and the Crows needed protection, never mind that Sioux raids against the Crows had been going on for decades.

On December 6, 1875, President Ulysses S. Grant issued an order that was basically a declaration of war. All Sioux living in the unceded territory of the Powder River country had to move onto agencies by January 31, 1876. If they didn't, the Army would come after them.

The winter of 1876–77 was brutally cold. Even though game was scarce, Crazy Horse seldom left his lodge to hunt. Black Shawl's cough had worsened with the frigid temperatures and biting winds. By the Moon of the Trees Popping, January, 1876, Crazy Horse was desperate.

Placing a pile of crossed brush in front of their lodge door to let people know that he and Black Shawl were away, Crazy Horse made a bed of warm robes on his travois. Riding his pony, he pulled Black Shawl over the snow to the Medicine Water lake (now Lake De Smet) where he built a sweat lodge. He had heard that a sweat brought on by throwing ice from the lake onto red-hot rocks would cure the white man's disease of tuberculosis. Both Crazy Horse and Black Shawl must have been well satisfied with their efforts. When they returned to their village near Bear Butte two weeks later, Black Shawl was riding her own pony and leading a pack mule loaded with game that Crazy Horse had killed.

Soon after their arrival back in camp, a runner from the Red Cloud Agency rode in. If Crazy Horse didn't bring his people into the agency by the end of the Moon of the Trees Popping, January, the runner said, the Army would come after them. Meeting with the runner in the council lodge, Crazy Horse quietly smoked his small pipe as Black Twin, one of his head men, spoke for him. Our people can't possibly move almost one hundred miles to the Red Cloud Agency in such deep snow and cold, Black Twin explained. Besides, this is Oglala country and no one can tell us where to go or when.

As if to mock the order, after the runner had left, Crazy Horse had his people pack up and travel almost two hundred miles north to join Sitting Bull and his Hunkpapas. (Sitting Bull had rejected the government's offer, too. Perhaps he would come in later, he said, like next summer.)

It was obvious to both the hostiles and the Army that the line had been drawn. And the stakes were high. For the Sioux, it meant preserving their way of life. For the whites it meant gaining millions of acres of land. Only war would decide the outcome.

CHAPTER 23

By 1875 there were more than ten thousand Sioux friendlies living on the agencies, while there were less than three thousand Sioux hostiles still out. All that changed in 1876. Everyone knew that a big fight with the Army was coming and some of the young men on the agencies had never been in a fight or earned war honors. Realizing this, Crazy Horse and Sitting Bull sent runners into the agencies early in the Moon of the Sore Eyes, February, with an irresistible challenge. "Come—there will be good fighting this year, plenty of coup and enough American horses for everybody! Come and bring guns."

Few young braves could refuse such an offer. For years they had heard of Crazy Horse and Sitting Bull and now was their chance to see the two war leaders for themselves and ride with them into battle. Plus, this promised to be the grandest Sioux get-together ever . . . and the last. The agency Sioux weren't fooling themselves that in the end they would defeat the Army but they could certainly have the time of their lives in the trying. In the Moon When the Grain Comes Up, March, 1876, the Sioux began leaving the agencies by the hundreds.

By the Moon of the Birth of Calves, April, Oglalas, Hunkpapas, Brulés, Blackfeet-Sioux, Sans Arcs, even Santee Sioux from the Missouri River, along with Cheyennes, some Arapahoes and Assiniboines had joined Crazy Horse and Sitting Bull in the Powder River country. The encampment of well over one thousand lodges was so large that it was impossible to see from end to end. With many of the people having come from the agencies where guns were more available, almost half of the some three thousand warriors had guns.

Crazy Horse was happy to see his friend He Dog and his followers return to the camp circle. Only a month earlier, He Dog had told Crazy Horse that his women were afraid and his children couldn't run away from the soldiers through the deep snow. He was going to take his people into the Red Cloud Agency, along with a party of Cheyennes. As always, Crazy Horse hadn't questioned his friend's decision but his heart had been heavy. A fellow shirt-wearer and lance-bearer, He Dog was one of Crazy Horse's oldest friends. Many years later, He Dog recalled: "I and Crazy Horse were born in the same year and at the same season of the year. We grew up together in the same band, played together, courted the girls together, and fought together."

As they had made their way south toward the Red Cloud Agency, He Dog and his people had been spotted by Crows scouting for General George Crook, known to the hostiles as Three Stars. When the scouts saw He Dog's pony, they had assumed that his good friend, Crazy Horse, was with him as usual and Crazy Horse, second only to Sitting Bull, was the prize to catch. Serving under Three Stars Crook, Colonel J. J. Reynolds had ordered an immediate attack. But He Dog's people had escaped, counterattacked and even recovered their pony herd that the soldiers had captured. Quickly turning around, He Dog had led his people back to Crazy Horse's camp.

Because the encampment grew ever larger, it was necessary to move every few days to have enough game and firewood, as well as grass for the thousands of ponies. By the time the last of the moving column reached a new campground, those who had arrived first had already put up their tipis, cooked and eaten their evening meal. What a glorious gathering it was. The buffalo, deer and elk hunting had never been better. The feasting and dancing and visiting continued day and night. Children raced their ponies and played their games, young adults courted in their blankets, oldsters renewed friendships and warriors boasted of what they would do in the fight to come.

Although the festivities must have reminded Crazy Horse of the happy times he had spent at Bear Butte as a boy, this summer was different. This summer he was second in command of the greatest Sioux war party ever assembled. Unlike the agency Sioux, neither he nor Sitting Bull anticipated defeat.

To prepare himself, Crazy Horse withdrew from all the merry-making. From time to time, he fasted, hoping for a vision that would tell him what to do. For two days he stared unmoving at Paha Sapa waiting for a sign. He even traveled to where the soldiers were camped to get a look at their guns and their white tents scattered like snow over the ground. When he returned, he brought with him a calf's skin from the soldiers' herd. Black Shawl stitched the red calfskin, with its white spots like the hail spots of his vision, into a war cape that would fly from his shoulders as he rode into battle.

While Crazy Horse prepared himself in private for the coming conflict, Sitting Bull, who at forty-five was no longer a fighting warrior, prepared his people. As head war chief, he sat in on councils, sent his men into Paha Sapa to steal guns and horses and sang songs to put heart into his warriors. And in the Moon of the Ripe Juneberries, June, he performed what forever after would be known as Sitting Bull's Sun Dance.

As tradition demanded, virgins cut down the "enemy," the tree that would serve as the sacred Sun Dance pole. After warriors counted coup on the tree, it was carried to the leafy bower that was the Dance lodge where it was dedicated and decorated. As the people gathered, a buffalo head was placed on an altar facing the sacred pole. To begin the ceremonies that would bring buffalo for the summer hunt or fulfill a vow made during the year, several warriors danced the Sun Dance. With skewers piercing their breasts or backs, the warriors blew on their eagle-bone whistles, stared up at the sun and danced. They circled and leapt and jerked until the skewers, which were attached by rawhide ropes to the sacred pole, were torn from their flesh in a gush of bright blood.

After the warriors had been helped back to their tipis, Sitting Bull, who had already been purified in a sweat lodge, stepped forward. In return for plentiful game and a happy life of strength and power for the Sioux, Sitting Bull pledged to give his flesh to Wakan Tanka. Naked to the waist, with his chest and back already scarred from previous Sun Dances, he sat against the sacred pole as his nephew cut out fifty pieces of flesh from each of his arms. With the blood flowing from his wounds, Sitting Bull stood up, faced the sun and began to

127

dance around the sacred pole. He danced all that day and into the night. He danced for eighteen hours before he fainted.

When he recovered, he spoke in a low voice to one of his head men, Black Moon, who, in turn, repeated his words to the waiting people. "Sitting Bull wishes to announce that he just heard a voice from above saying, 'I give you these because they have no ears.' He looked up and saw soldiers and some Indians on horseback coming down like grasshoppers, with their heads down and their hats falling off. They were falling right into our camp."

The people were jubilant. No holy man had to tell them what Sitting Bull's dream meant. The soldiers were going to attack their encampment, and in the battle that followed, the soldiers would all be killed. Hoka hey, let the fighting begin!

CHAPTER 24

Only three days after Sitting Bull's Sun Dance, Cheyenne scouts galloped into the hostiles' encampment on Ash Creek (now Reno Creek). Three Stars Crook was marching north toward them with one thousand men, plus more than two hundred Crow, Shoshoni and Pawnee warriors. The head chiefs quickly held a council. Although Crazy Horse seldom spoke out, in view of Sitting Bull's vision of soldiers falling into camp, he knew that he had to make his voice heard. The people's safety must come first, he said. Half or more of the warriors should stay behind to protect the people, while he, Crazy Horse, would lead the other fifteen hundred warriors against Three Stars. The head men agreed. Weak as he still was from his Sun Dance, even Sitting Bull planned to accompany the war party.

That very day, Crazy Horse led his warriors in an all-night march through the divide in the Wolf Mountains to Rosebud Creek. At dawn on June 17, 1876, Crazy Horse had his men stop to let their ponies rest and graze while they dressed and painted for war and armed themselves. Because he was determined to find Three Stars before Three Stars found them, within a few hours Crazy Horse had his war party on the move again.

And find Three Stars he did. Crawling to the top of a high hill, Crazy Horse spotted some six hundred of Three Stars' soldiers, as well as all of the Army's Crow, Shoshoni and Pawnee allies, scattered on either side of Rosebud Creek below him. All of a sudden, a party of Crow scouts appeared over the brow of the hill. They saw not only Crazy Horse but his massed war party as well. They turned and galloped back down the hill, shouting the alarm the whole way, "Lakota! Lakota!"

At that, there was no holding back the eager warriors. As Crazy Horse led the charge, a voice cried out, "Take courage! This is a good day to die! Think of the children and the helpless at home!" The battle had begun.

Although Rosebud Creek ran through the middle of a mile-wide valley with bluffs on either side, rocks, trees and bushes broke up the terrain. It was pretty much every man for himself with neither Crazy Horse nor Three Stars in total command of his forces. Crazy Horse fought as one more courageous warrior among many courageous warriors, while Sitting Bull, who could barely sit his pony, called out encouragement.

The hostiles never let up as they knocked the soldiers from their horses with war clubs, lances, knives and even guns. Dismounting, killing and leaping back on their ponies, they charged repeatedly in a dust cloud so dense that it was hard to see. Fearless and brave as always, the Sioux and Cheyenne warriors fought as if a new life force had seized them. There was little of the old hovering and circling at a safe distance and

130

almost no racing back to their own lines after a quick dash in to count coup or take a scalp.

Surprised by the warriors' new offensive tactics, Three Stars marshalled his troops and counterattacked. Although he came close to succeeding, his men were turned back. "Crazy Horse, Bad Heart Bull, Black Deer, Kicking Bear, and Good Weasel rallied the Sioux, turned the charge, and got the soldiers on the run," He Dog's brother Short Bull reported. "When these five commenced to rally their men, that was as far as the soldiers got . . . Crazy Horse used good judgment in this Rosebud fight."

When the fighting slackened off around noon, Three Stars sent Colonel Anson Mills and eight troops of cavalry downstream to find Crazy Horse's encampment and destroy it. But when Mills' Crow scouts saw that the valley ahead narrowed into a steep canyon, they refused to go on. This was Crazy Horse they were fighting and they knew Crazy Horse's fondness for ambushes all too well.

Meanwhile, Crazy Horse had watched Mills and his men ride off. As soon as they were out of sight, he massed his warriors for an attack on Three Stars' left flank and rear. Again, it was the Crows who saved the day for the Army. Realizing what Crazy Horse was up to, they warned Three Stars, who ordered an officer to ride after Mills and bring him back. The sudden appearance of Mills and his cavalry on Crazy Horse's own flank and rear scattered the hostile forces. With that, the six-hour Battle of the Rosebud was over.

Crazy Horse led his war party back to their encampment on Ash Creek, while Three Stars and his men headed south in what amounted to a retreat. Although twenty-one of Crazy Horse's warriors were killed, the numbers didn't tell the whole story.

In the battle that the Sioux called The Fight with Three

Stars, Crazy Horse's men had given up their old strategy of striking and running, as well as riding out alone to prove their bravery and win honors. Instead, they had charged into the fray, riding massed together when they could, breaking up the soldiers' lines and attacking aggressively over and over. Crazy Horse must have felt a deep sense of satisfaction and pride. Well aware that this one battle didn't win the war, he knew that his warriors' new spirit would serve them well in the days ahead.

CHAPTER 25

June 25, 1876, was hot, windless and dusty, especially dusty. It hadn't rained for a long time and seven thousand people with all their pony herds raised a lot of dust. At least the winding Little Bighorn River in the valley where the Sioux and Northern Cheyennes had set up their encampment bubbled clear and cool and there was relief from the sun under the cottonwood trees that lined its banks. (The Sioux called the Little Bighorn River the Greasy Grass because their ponies grew fat and sleek on its lush spring grasses.)

It was a lazy kind of day, with the children splashing in the river as swallows darted overhead. The older girls kept an eye on the swimmers, while the boys tended the huge pony herds west of camp. Some of the men were out hunting and some were simply loafing in the shade of their rolled-up tipis. The women chatted among themselves as they worked on hides or gathered wild turnips out on the prairie to dry for winter soups.

A week had passed week since The Fight with Three Stars. Although the women had keened and mourned as they left the death scaffolds of their loved ones behind, the camp had to keep on the move. Heralds had been posted along the line of march to direct everyone to their proper place in the new encampment just west of the Little Bighorn River.

As all sacred things were round, the sun, moon, earth and horizon, the three-mile-long camp was made up of seven circles of tipis. Each tribal circle had its appointed place, with each band in its appointed place within its tribal circle and every tipi in its assigned place within the band. (Hunkpatila, which was Crazy Horse's band, meant End-of-Circle, the place of honor at the entrance to the Oglala circle.) The circles, as well as every tipi door flap, opened to the east to welcome the sun that brought the day. The Hunkpapas were posted at the upper, or southern, end of camp, while the Cheyennes were posted at the lower, or northern end, the two positions of greatest responsibility and danger.

Although June 25 may have been a lazy day for everyone else, it wasn't a lazy day for Crazy Horse. The only time he left his command post in the center of the Oglala circle was to consult with the Hunkpapa chiefs, Sitting Bull and Gall, and the Northern Cheyenne chief, Two Moon. (Sitting Bull and Gall's command post was in the center of the Hunkpapa circle, just as Two Moon's command post was centered in the Cheyenne circle.)

With his scouts coming and going constantly, Crazy Horse knew that Three Stars Crook and his men had retreated south after their battle on Rosebud Creek and were no longer a threat. But a new regiment of more than six hundred cavalrymen was now approaching the Little Bighorn valley.

Crazy Horse may have known how many soldiers were

coming and what route they were taking, but he didn't know that this regiment was Long Hair Custer's 7th Cavalry. This was the same Long Hair who had attacked the Cheyennes at Washita, the same Long Hair whom Crazy Horse had fought at the Battle of the Yellowstone, the same Long Hair who had led the march through Paha Sapa on the Thieves' Road.

Crazy Horse also didn't know that Long Hair had divided his regiment into three battalions. One battalion, under Major Marcus Reno, with 140 men, was to cross the Little Bighorn River and attack the upper, Hunkpapa end of camp. A second battalion, under Captain Frederick Benteen, 125 men strong, was ordered to march west-southwest and engage any hostiles whom it might find. Meanwhile, Long Hair, at the head of about 225 men, planned to ride north along the bluffs. Escorted by 130 men, the slow-moving train of pack mules carrying ammunition, food, tents, blankets and feed for the horses was a good distance behind the others.

Early in the afternoon, when everything in the encampment was at its most peaceful, a tower of dust was seen advancing from the south. A cry went up, "Soldiers coming here! Soldiers coming here!" Reno's battalion, which had already forded the Little Bighorn River, was riding straight for the Hunkpapa circle. Even Crazy Horse, who was visiting three miles away in the Cheyenne camp, was caught by surprise. Chief Red Horse described what happened next: "We gave directions immediately for every Indian to take his horse and arms; for the women and children to mount their horses and get out of the way, and for the young men to go and meet the troops."

Foremost on Crazy Horse's mind was Sitting Bull's vision of soldiers falling into camp. The moment had arrived! Leaping on his pinto, he raced through the encampment. All was

135

choking dust, noise and chaos. Runners shouted out the alarm, women grabbed up their babies, little ones ran to find their mothers, old people hobbled along on sticks as the elders directed everyone to the safety of the lower Cheyenne end of camp. Warriors, who caught up the first good ponies from the herds that were being driven in, mounted with war whoops and headed south to the scene of the action.

By the time Crazy Horse reached the Hunkpapa end of camp with his war party behind him, Reno's men had already begun firing. Some of the Hunkpapa tipis had been ripped apart by bullets, others had been knocked down, while still others were burning. Only one hundred or so warriors were holding off the soldiers, waiting until they were sure that the women and children were safe before they charged. Having first made certain that his old mother was out of harm's way, Sitting Bull, seated on his black and white war pony, rallied his men.

As soon as Crazy Horse (stripped to his breechcloth and wearing a single feather in his hair) rode up on his pinto, the impatient warriors let out a roar. "Crazy Horse is coming! Crazy Horse is coming!" Now, with the arrival of their war leader, they could charge, attack, shoot, fight to the death. But the scouts had reported that there were many more soldiers than just these. Not one bullet must be wasted.

"Be strong, friends! Make them shoot three times fast, so their guns will stick and you can knock them down with your clubs!" Crazy Horse called out as he rode up and down in front of the soldiers' skirmish line, drawing their fire but never being hit.

By this time the soldiers had dismounted and were shooting long range. Not only had they marched hard for days, but they had also marched through the night and they were

136

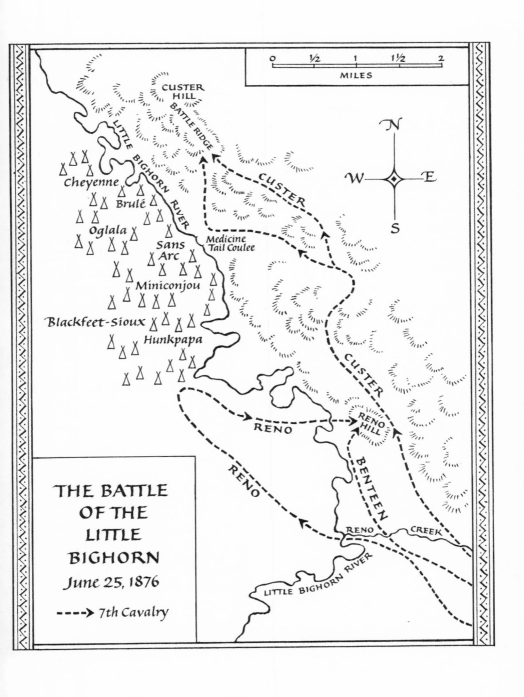

CUSTER HILL
BATTLE RIDGE

CUSTER

LITTLE BIGHORN RIVER

Cheyenne

Brulé

Oglala

Sans
Arc

Miniconjou

Blackfeet-Sioux

Hunkpapa

Medicine
Tail Coulee

N
W · E
S

CUSTER

RENO

RENO
HILL

RENO

BENTEEN

RENO CREEK

LITTLE BIGHORN RIVER

0   ½   1   1½   2
MILES

THE BATTLE
OF THE
LITTLE
BIGHORN
June 25, 1876

----▸ 7th Cavalry

exhausted. Sitting Bull described their fatigue. "They were brave men but they were too tired. When they rode up, their horses were tired and they were tired. When they got off from their horses they could not stand firmly on their feet . . . Some of them staggered under the weight of their guns."

The warriors, who took advantage of the cavalrymen having dismounted, rode the length of the soldiers' skirmish line, galloped around the battalion's left flank and came up on their rear. Overwhelmed, the soldiers turned back toward the river and raced for the protection of the cottonwood groves along its banks. But many of the warriors had already forded the river and, in an effort to save their ammunition as Crazy Horse had commanded, were already firing arrows from the other side.

Realizing that their position was hopeless, Reno ordered a retreat. Panicked, his men forded the river on their horses, struggled up the bank and headed toward the safety of the bluffs beyond. But the warriors were all over them. The Hunkpapa White Bull summed up what happened: "Then the Indians charged them. They used war clubs and gun barrels, shooting arrows into them, riding them down. It was like a buffalo hunt."

Forty of Reno's cavalrymen were killed and thirteen wounded in the fighting that lasted little more than an hour. The survivors, who reached the treeless bluffs and scrambled into a defensive position, were joined soon after by Major Benteen's battalion and then later by the pack train.

Although the warriors were prepared to finish off Reno's men, Crazy Horse had to plan ahead. He now knew that more than two hundred soldiers were riding north along the bluffs where the women and children and helpless ones had taken refuge. Every available man was needed to protect the people.

138

"Hoka hey!" he called out. "It is a good day to fight! It is a good day to die! Strong hearts, brave hearts, to the front! Weak hearts and cowards to the rear."

With that challenge, Crazy Horse accomplished the impossible. He persuaded his warriors to ride away from a fight that they were sure to win. And if there were any weak hearts or cowards following Crazy Horse that day, they weren't visible. As the war party of mostly Oglalas and Cheyennes thundered through the empty camp, they knocked over pots and kettles and startled stray dogs rooting through the food stores. Alerted to the danger, the men who had been out hunting had raced back and now joined Crazy Horse's war party.

As always, Crazy Horse's first concern was the safety of the people. When word spread that another battle was about to take place, this time to the north, the old men and boys had herded everyone out on the flat about a half-mile west of the river. Crazy Horse's father, Worm, and his uncle, Little Hawk, were there, quieting and calming the people. Sitting Bull was there, too, seated on his war pony. Once Crazy Horse was assured that the people were taken care of, he put his heart and mind to the battle ahead.

Some of Long Hair's cavalry had already started down Medicine Tail Coulee, a ravine that led to the river opposite the Sans Arc and Miniconjou circles where the banks were low and the water was shallow enough to ford. The soldiers never made it to the river. Waving their blankets and shouting, Gall and hundreds of Hunkpapa warriors rode out to meet them. Under Gall's fierce attack, the soldiers beat a retreat back up the ravine to try and rejoin their battalion. But Gall and his Hunkpapas charged after them, scattering their forces all over the treeless hillside.

Through the dust and the gunsmoke, Crazy Horse saw that the retreating soldiers were trying to reach their comrades on

139

the bluffs. Maybe they planned to take up a defensive position the way Reno and Benteen's battalions had done four miles to the south. Or maybe they planned to swing around behind the bluffs in a flanking maneuver to attack the encampment from the rear. Either way, Crazy Horse knew that he had to stop them. Instead of a frontal attack as the soldiers probably expected, he would circle around and attack the soldiers from *their* rear.

Leading his war party across the Little Bighorn River, Crazy Horse swept in a wide arc around to the back of the ridge. The ponies had galloped hard up to the crest of the ridge and they paused a moment to get second wind. Crazy Horse, with his red calfskin cape motionless in the still air, was poised at the head of his war party, his Winchester rifle held lightly in his hand.

What a sight it must have been for the soldiers, who were desperately fighting off Gall and his Hunkpapas on the hillside below. Behind Crazy Horse ranged one thousand warriors, stripped to breechcloths and moccasins, their magnificent eagle-feathered war bonnets trailing down their backs, their faces and bodies painted in brilliant colors. Using their knees to guide their ponies, with their shields on their left arms, they held a variety of weapons—guns, war clubs and bows, as well as lances that glistened in the sun. Their ponies, fat and strong from the forage of the Greasy Grass, were painted, too, with their tails tied up for battle.

Once again Crazy Horse and Long Hair Custer faced each other. Because Custer had probably heard by now that Crazy Horse dressed plainly and wore a single feather in his hair, he might have recognized him. Custer, on the other hand, had cut his hair short and grown a straggly beard so it was doubtful that Crazy Horse would have picked him out from among the others. For an instant, the scene was frozen in time and then the instant exploded.

"Hi-yi-yi!" the chiefs yelled. The warriors echoed their cry, "Hi-yi-yi!"

With that, Crazy Horse led the attack in a roar of war whoops, shrill yelps, the shriek of eagle-bone whistles and guns firing. The Cheyenne chief, Two Moon, who had followed Crazy Horse up the hill, described the action: "The shooting was quick, quick. Pop—pop—pop very fast. Some of the soldiers were down on their knees, some standing . . . The smoke was like a great cloud, and everywhere the Sioux went the dust rose like smoke. We circled all around them— swirling like water round a stone. We shoot, we ride fast, we shoot again. Soldiers drop, and horses fall on them."

It was all over in not much more than an hour. The smell of gunpowder lingered in the haze of dust and smoke that made the bright day as dark as night. Long Hair and his men had fought courageously but with Crazy Horse and Two Moon attacking from the north and west, and Gall attacking from the south, not one of Long Hair's men survived. And it was never known who killed Lieutenant Colonel George Armstrong Custer. Spotted Blackbird recalled, "If we could have seen where each bullet landed, we might have known. But hundreds of bullets were flying that day."

As for Crazy Horse, one of the Arapahoes who had fought in the battle declared: "Crazy Horse, the Sioux Chief, was the bravest man I ever saw. He rode closest to the soldiers, yelling to his warriors. All the soldiers were shooting at him, but he was never hit."

Crazy Horse was more than brave. Although Sitting Bull, Gall and Two Moon had been in on the planning, and all but Sitting Bull had been in on the fighting, it was Crazy Horse

141

who had been the heart and soul of the battle. Over the years, the silent, modest Oglala had risen to near-mystical status as a warrior. Because of that status, he had been able to convince his war party to hoard their ammunition during the Reno fight. He had been able to lead his men away from a battle that they knew they could win. Under his leadership, no young warrior had broken rank to count coup or try to win honors on his own. And in the end, Crazy Horse had outthought and outmaneuvered the best that the United States Army could throw against him.

Almost twenty years before, when Crazy Horse had been a young man, the Sioux head men had met in council at Bear Butte. Although they had pledged to fight the white takeover of their land, their promises and vows to unite for the common good had come to nothing. But when the soldiers had fallen into camp on this hot June day in 1876, Crazy Horse had been the guiding spirit behind a unified and disciplined fighting force that had seen the dream of Bear Butte become a reality.

CHAPTER 26

The Battle of the Little Bighorn wasn't quite over. Reno and Benteen's battalions and the men from the pack train were still holed up on top of the bluff. Leaving the scene of their victory over Long Hair and his battalion, the war party rode four miles south to take out what was left of the 7th Cavalry. But the soldiers and packers were in a protected defensive position. Although the warriors kept them pinned down for three hours, there was no way to get past the soldiers' firepower. When darkness fell, a few guards were posted, while the rest of the warriors rode back to the encampment to join in mourning the forty or so of their own men who had been killed that day.

During the night, the soldiers and packers dug shallow entrenchments and threw up makeshift barricades. All the next morning and into the afternoon, the warriors kept up their firing but they still couldn't penetrate the soldiers' defenses. And then scouts brought word that many more soldiers were marching up the Little Bighorn River from the north. Enough was enough. It was time for the Sioux and Cheyennes to move on.

With criers shouting orders to march out, the people broke camp early in the evening of June 26. As they left, they set fire to the dry prairie grass so that the soldiers' horses would have no forage if they tried to follow. In a long line of march, the huge encampment headed toward the Bighorn Mountains. Behind them, they left the survivors of the 7th Cavalry to tell a shocked nation of the death of Custer and more than 260 of his men at the Battle of the Little Bighorn.

On the fourth night after the battle, when the mourning rituals for their fallen warriors had ended, the Sioux and Cheyennes celebrated their victory with feasting, dancing and singing. Black Elk recalled some of their kill-songs.

> *Long Hair has never returned,*
> *So his woman is crying, crying.*
> *Looking over here, she cries.*
>
> *Long Hair, where he lies nobody knows.*
> *Crying, they seek him.*
> *He lies over here.*
>
> *Long Hair, guns I had none.*
> *You brought me many. I thank you!*
> *You make me laugh!*

For most of the Moon of the Ripening Chokecherries, July, the Sioux and Cheyennes camped together, going into the Bighorn Mountains for lodgepoles and game and then return-ing to the prairie for more feasting and dancing and singing. But it was hard to find enough game for such a large encamp-ment and many of the families began to drift back to the agencies. With the Sioux and Cheyennes splitting up into smaller camps, Crazy Horse and his people headed east toward Paha Sapa and Bear Butte to fatten up their ponies for the winter ahead. As they traveled, they burned the prairie grass behind them until rolling billows of black smoke filled the summer sky.

Camped with his people near Bear Butte, Crazy Horse was very much aware that white miners still overran Paha Sapa. Sometimes alone, and sometimes with small war parties, he raided the miners' camps, bringing back goods and supplies. Because he never forgot the children, he once returned with two large sacks of raisins. Gathering up the little ones, he held out the sacks for them to enjoy the sweet raisins that he had enjoyed as a boy during the summers when he and his family had camped along the Holy Road.

On other expeditions into Paha Sapa, Crazy Horse went by himself to pick off solitary miners silently with arrows or his war club. "My friend," a worried He Dog warned, "you are past the foolish years of the wild young warrior; you belong to the people now and must think of them, nor give them such uneasiness."

He Dog didn't understand. Two victories against the whites didn't end the war and there was still much to be done. Crazy Horse could never let up on his mission to take back the sacred land that the whites had promised to the Sioux "as long as grass should grow and water flow."

But unknown to Crazy Horse, the country was in such an uproar over the deaths of Custer and his men that Congress voted to give the Army everything that it asked for. Two new forts were to be built on the Yellowstone River and plans were made to send many more troops west. In late July, all the agencies were taken out of the Indian Bureau in the

Department of the Interior where they had been since 1849 and turned back to the military. With that decision, the friendlies living on the agencies were now official prisoners of war and all their arms and ponies were taken from them.

In the Moon of the Yellow Leaves, September, 1876, General Three Stars Crook headed out with two thousand men to find Crazy Horse and his people. But they soon became lost north of the Black Hills in the mud and mire of endless rain on what was later called the "starvation march." With his men driven to eating their horses and mules, Three Stars sent Captain Anson Mills and 150 men south into the Black Hills to pick up supplies and food.

At dawn on September 9, Mills, who had called the Sioux "the best cavalry soldiers on earth," happened upon thirty-seven lodges of Brulés camped near Slim Buttes. It didn't matter that the Brulés had just left Crazy Horse's encampment to head back to the Spotted Tail Agency. Mills attacked anyway, driving the people up to the bluffs. As the famished soldiers pounced on the camp's food stores, the Brulés sent runners to Crazy Horse for help.

By the time Crazy Horse and two hundred warriors arrived at Slim Buttes, Three Stars and his 1,850 men had already reinforced Mills. Hopelessly outnumbered, Crazy Horse had no choice but to retreat. Although Crazy Horse and his war party harassed Three Stars' troops as they headed for the safety of the Black Hills, they weren't able to inflict much damage. Perhaps it was during this encounter at Slim Buttes that Crazy Horse realized for the first time that the Army's numbers were soaring at the same time that his warrior-strength was dwindling. Other Oglalas, who also must have sensed the balance shifting, called the battle at Slim Buttes the Fight Where We Lost the Black Hills.

146

While Crazy Horse continued to make quick strikes against the whites in Paha Sapa, the United States government was busy stealing not only Paha Sapa, but the Powder River and Bighorn countries as well. Since the government couldn't buy the land or win it in battle, either, officials in Washington decided to take it by blackmail. In the Moon of the Ripe Plums, August, 1876, Congress passed a bill declaring that no more food or provisions would be given to anyone on the agencies until the Sioux signed a treaty giving up the Black Hills and the Powder River and Bighorn countries.

By September 19, 1876, with their people on the agencies threatened with starvation, Red Cloud, Spotted Tail and other agency head men had no choice but to touch the pen to the treaty that the commission from Washington presented to them. Speaking for all the Sioux, Chief Standing Elk's tongue-lashing to the commissioners summed up Sioux bitterness. "Your words are like a man knocking me in the head with a stick," he declared. "Whatever we do, wherever we go, we are expected to say yes! yes! yes!—and when we don't agree at once to what you ask of us in council, you always say, You won't get anything to eat! You won't get anything to eat!"

Early that same fall, Crazy Horse led his people west to the Powder River country. Black Elk told of their suffering. "We went back deep into our country, and most of the land was black from the fire, and the bison had gone away . . . a hard winter came on early. It snowed much; game was hard to find, and it was a hungry time for us. Ponies died, and we ate them."

It was an especially hard time for Crazy Horse. Not only did he have to witness the suffering of his people, but news reached him, too, that Paha Sapa and the Powder River and Bighorn countries were gone. Signed away by agency chiefs, even Red Cloud and his uncle, Spotted Tail! But he, Crazy Horse, had agreed to nothing. This was his rightful land and this was where he and his people would live.

But the treaty did more than give away Sioux land. It also made Crazy Horse and anyone else who refused to come into the agencies, enemy aliens. On November 25, 1876, Three Stars Crook, with 2,200 men, attacked the Cheyenne villages of Dull Knife and Little Wolf not far from the Bighorn Mountains. Although the four hundred or so Cheyenne warriors fought gallantly in what was sometimes hand-to-hand combat, Three Stars' men killed forty Cheyenne men, women and children, captured seven hundred ponies and set fire to all the tipis and everything in them. The survivors struggled on foot through the snow for two weeks until they found Crazy Horse's camp. In weather that saw the temperature plummet to thirty degrees below zero, eleven babies froze to death in their mothers' arms.

Desperate as they were themselves, Crazy Horse and his people took in the Cheyennes and gave them shelter and food. "We helped the Cheyennes the best we could. We hadn't much ourselves," Short Bull said modestly. A Cheyenne warrior expressed it better. "Oh, how generous were the Oglalas!"

But by the middle of the Moon of Frost in the Tipi, December, Crazy Horse knew in his heart that it was time to give up. His people were starving in one of the coldest winters in memory. His wife, Black Shawl, was sick with tuberculosis and he had only about five hundred warriors left, with few guns and almost no ammunition. He must put his warrior-pride aside. The people, his people, had to come first.

CHAPTER 27

Every fort commander wanted the honor of having Crazy Horse surrender to him. Colonel Nelson Miles, whom the Sioux called Bear Coat because of the bearskin coat he wore, sent runners to Crazy Horse's camp with promises that he would treat both Crazy Horse and his people fairly if they came into his post on the Tongue River.

Heartsick at what he knew he had to do, Crazy Horse led the six hundred lodges of Sioux and those Cheyennes still with him to Bear Coat's Tongue River Cantonment, later named Fort Keogh. On December 16, 1876, after making camp, Crazy Horse selected eight warriors to act as peace envoys. He watched from a distance as his men rode toward the fort carrying a white flag of surrender and leading stolen American horses as a peace offering. But when the fort's Crow scouts saw the Sioux coming in, they leapt on their ponies before the soldiers could stop them. Giving war whoops and shouting, they rode out and attacked, leaving five of Crazy Horse's peace envoys dead in the snow.

Nothing had changed! White promises broken again! Crazy Horse immediately gathered up his people and led them back into the brutal Plains winter. Luther Standing Bear later commented: "Crazy Horse saw nothing, knew nothing but treachery from the white man. He felt himself above dealing with men who knew no honor. As by all such men Crazy Horse was sincerely hated and feared."

Several times during the next few weeks, families packed up and tried to steal away to the agencies. Much as Crazy Horse hated to prevent his people from making their own life-choices, he stopped them from leaving, either by the threat of force or by having their ponies shot. Perhaps he thought that they, too, would be killed as his five warriors had been killed. Or it may have been that he didn't believe that they could survive the long journey in the snow. It was even possible that Crazy Horse knew that Bear Coat Miles was on his way after them with troops and howitzers.

In the Moon of the Trees Popping, January, 1877, Bear Coat Miles found them. On both January 1 and 3, 1877, Crazy Horse and Bear Coat's forces had a couple of minor skirmishes in snow that was at least two feet deep, with the temperature hovering around zero. Four days later, the hostiles and Bear Coat's advance scouts had a hard fight during which a Cheyenne warrior and seven Cheyenne women and children were captured.

The following morning, January 8, Crazy Horse and his Sioux and Cheyenne war party rode up the Wolf Mountain hills and ridges. Looking down to the valley below, they could see Bear Coat's troops eating breakfast in a grove of trees. A warrior called out for them to eat well as this would be their last meal.

With that, the hostiles charged into the troops and the fight

150

that was called the Battle of Wolf Mountain was on. Although there were twice as many warriors as soldiers, the infantry's firepower, plus their two howitzers, made the difference. After five hours, Crazy Horse was forced to withdraw up the Tongue River valley. As Bear Coat Miles and his men headed out in pursuit, they happened upon Crazy Horse's encampment. After destroying all the hostiles' food supplies, the soldiers again gave chase until more snow, followed by rain, drove them back to their post.

Although Crazy Horse and his people stayed out, the loss of their food stores was devastating. With many of the starving children suffering from frozen limbs, Crazy Horse no longer had the heart to prevent families from leaving his camp and going into the agencies.

Sometime in the middle of the Moon of the Trees Popping, January, 1877, Sitting Bull and a number of his Hunkpapa warriors arrived from the north with more than fifty boxes of ammunition and many new blankets. And a plan. Sitting Bull urged Crazy Horse to gather his people together and flee with him and his Hunkpapas to Canada. "We can find peace in the land of the Grandmother [Queen Victoria]," Sitting Bull said. "We can sleep sound there, our women and children can lie down and feel safe."

But Crazy Horse knew that Canada was even colder than the Powder River country. He couldn't ask his people to endure more suffering. Besides, the Powder River country was his country and he would die, if need be, to defend it.

"My friend," he replied to Sitting Bull, "the soldiers are everywhere; the Indians are getting scattered so that the soldiers can capture or kill them all. This is the end. All the time these soldiers will keep hunting us down. Some day I shall be killed. Well, all right. I am going south to get mine!"

That winter took its toll on everyone, especially Crazy Horse. Black Elk remembered Crazy Horse's response to their desperate situation. "After that the people noticed that Crazy Horse was queerer than ever. He hardly ever stayed in camp. People would find him out alone in the cold . . . People wondered if he ate anything at all. Once my father found him out alone like that, and he said to my father: 'Uncle, you have noticed me the way I act. But do not worry; there are caves and holes for me to live in, and out here the spirits may help me. I am making plans for the good of my people.' "

But what was best for his people, to stay out or take them in? And if he did take them in, which agency should they go to? While Crazy Horse pondered his choices, all the military commanders were sending out messengers with gifts and food to bribe the celebrated warrior into their forts.

Red Cloud's nephew, Sword, who had once been a fellow shirt-wearer, appeared at Crazy Horse's camp on the Little Bighorn River with an offer from Three Stars Crook. If Crazy Horse and his people came in and handed over all their guns and ponies, they wouldn't be punished for the "Custer Massacre." Sword also gave Crazy Horse a gift of tobacco wrapped in red cloth. As was the Sioux custom, if the package was opened, it meant that the offer was accepted. (Crazy Horse didn't open the package.)

Shortly after, another messenger arrived at Crazy Horse's camp. Sent by Bear Coat Miles, this envoy not only carried a message similar to Sword's, but he also brought with him a Cheyenne woman who had been captured earlier as a token of good faith.

Three Stars Crook next arranged to have Crazy Horse's uncle, Spotted Tail, make the difficult journey through the snow to the Powder River country. To command Crazy

Horse's respect, Spotted Tail was accompanied by two hundred warriors and a pack train full of gifts. When the peace party arrived, Crazy Horse was out hunting, although he had left a message with his father, Worm, that he would bring his people in when the weather warmed up. Spotted Tail, in turn, left a message for Crazy Horse. If Crazy Horse surrendered to Three Stars at Camp Robinson, he would be given his own agency in the Powder River country.

Although many of his people had left for the agencies, including his cousin and long-time friend, the seven-foot-tall Miniconjou Touch-the-Clouds, Crazy Horse didn't make his decision until the Moon of the Birth of Calves, April, 1877. He chose to take his people into the Red Cloud Agency eighty miles east of Fort Laramie, close by Camp Robinson. Certainly Crazy Horse must have been influenced by the promise of his own agency in his beloved Powder River country. He had also counciled with his head men who had agreed with his choice. The old chief Iron Hawk told him: "You see all the people here are in rags, they all need clothing; we may as well go in."

Word quickly reached the military commander of the Red Cloud Agency, Lieutenant William Philo Clark, known to the Sioux as White Hat. On April 12, 1877, he sent Red Cloud out with seventy men and a pack train of food and gifts to greet Crazy Horse and escort him and his people in.

"All is well," Red Cloud assured Crazy Horse when they met. "Have no fear, come on in."

To signify that he was surrendering, Crazy Horse gave Red Cloud his shirt and spread out his blanket for Red Cloud to sit on. How strange this meeting must have seemed to the two warriors. Ten years before, they had been so powerful that they had forced the United States Army to abandon the three Bozeman Trail forts. Since then, both men had devoted themselves to the survival of their people, Red Cloud by cooperating with the whites and Crazy Horse by fighting them. Now Crazy Horse's world was in ruins. His life as a warrior was over. His country was gone. He had failed his people.

On May 6, 1877, Crazy Horse, the some nine hundred people who were still with him and their two thousand ponies approached Camp Robinson. When White Hat Clark rode out to greet them, Crazy Horse offered his left hand. *"Kola* [friend]," he said to White Hat, "I shake with this hand because my heart is on this side; the right hand does all manner of wickedness; I want this peace to last forever." Because Crazy Horse had never worn a war bonnet, He Dog stepped forward and, as a sign of surrender, gave White Hat his own war bonnet and war-shirt, as well as his pipe and beaded tobacco pouch.

After the brief ceremony, Crazy Horse and his people began the five-mile march to the camp itself. In proper military formation, Crazy Horse and his head men, He Dog, Little Big Man, Big Road and his uncle, Little Hawk, rode five abreast, with three hundred warriors riding behind them. Crazy Horse, who held his Winchester in his lap, had only a single hawk feather in his hair, with his long fur-wrapped braids falling over a simple buckskin shirt. Wearing their war bonnets and carrying their arms, all the others had painted their faces and bodies and ponies as if for war. The moving village, the women, children and old ones, followed the warriors, with the pony herds bringing up the rear in a procession that stretched for two miles. Thousands of agency Sioux lined their route for a glimpse of the legendary Crazy Horse, their hero, the greatest Oglala war leader of them all.

154

When Crazy Horse and his people came in sight of Camp Robinson, the chiefs started to sing their brave-heart song. The warriors picked it up and then the women and children joined in. As the valley filled with song, the agency Sioux began to sing, too. Suddenly, what was meant to be a march of surrender had become a triumphal parade and it told Crazy Horse everything that he needed to know.

The singing told Crazy Horse that his people knew that he had never given up fighting for their land no matter what the odds had been. It told him that his people knew that he had protected them and kept them free longer than any other Oglala leader. It told him that his people exulted in his victories over Fetterman, Three Stars Crook and Long Hair Custer. And he had given them back pride in themselves when they had been hunted and run down like wild game. Now the people, his people, were expressing their praise and gratitude for all the world to hear.

CHAPTER 28

Almost from the time that Crazy Horse surrendered in the Moon of the Thunderstorms, May, 1877, there was trouble at the Red Cloud Agency. Not that Crazy Horse wanted trouble. Far from it. "I came here for peace," he said. "No matter if my own relatives pointed a gun at my head and ordered me to change that word I would not change it."

Understandably, the officers and soldiers stationed at nearby Camp Robinson were fascinated by Crazy Horse, the man who had wiped out Custer and most of the 7th Cavalry. They visited him often on Little Cottonwood Creek, six miles from the Red Cloud Agency where he and his people had set up their village. Red Feather, Crazy Horse's brother-in-law, recalled: "All the white people came to see Crazy Horse and gave him presents and money. The other Indians at the agency got very jealous."

It wasn't the young warriors who were jealous. They, in fact, respected and looked up to Crazy Horse as the bravest of all the Oglalas. It was the head men, especially Red Cloud, who resented the attention showered on Crazy Horse. Red Cloud's first complaint was that Crazy Horse had bypassed the medicine man and taken his wife to the Camp Robinson doctor, Dr. V. T. McGillicuddy, to treat her tuberculosis.

Crazy Horse calmly replied that the medicine man hadn't helped Black Shawl and he was willing to try anything to cure her. During Black Shawl's treatment, Crazy Horse and Dr. McGillicuddy became friendly, although Crazy Horse would never allow the doctor to photograph him. "My friend, why should you wish to shorten my life by taking from me my shadow?" he asked.

Red Cloud was jealous, too, that the soldiers wanted Crazy Horse to meet with the Great White Father, the President. Because Red Cloud worried that Crazy Horse might be made head chief if he traveled to Washington, he spread rumors that Crazy Horse was about to break out and go on the warpath. The idea was ridiculous. Like everyone else, Crazy Horse had given up all his guns and ponies when he had surrendered.

Red Cloud needn't have worried. Crazy Horse had been promised his own agency if he came in and until that happened, he announced, he wasn't going anywhere. He had already picked out the perfect location where the water ran clear and the grass was good for both ponies and game. "First, I want them to place my agency on Beaver Creek west of the Black Hills," he said. "Then I will go to Washington."

That was not the way it worked, White Hat Clark explained. Crazy Horse could have his agency *after* he had seen the Great White Father.

But Crazy Horse had no interest in seeing the Great White Father. He replied that he "was not hunting for any Great

Father; his father was with him, and there was no Great Father between him and the Great Spirit.''

A month or so later, Crazy Horse changed his mind. It was clear that until he went to Washington he wasn't going to be given his own agency. And above all, he longed to be back in the country that he loved, to ride free and hunt game as he always had.

As soon as Crazy Horse agreed to go to Washington, the soldiers couldn't do enough for him. They promised that he could go on a buffalo hunt with his fellow Oglalas. They promised that he could be host at a huge buffalo feast. And of course he would be given his own agency when he returned.

It was all too much for Red Cloud. If Crazy Horse is allowed to have ponies and guns for a buffalo hunt, he'll use them to go on the warpath again, Red Cloud and his followers whispered to the whites. And it wasn't right that Crazy Horse should have the honor of hosting a feast when he had only come in two months before.

Crazy Horse's Brulé uncle, Spotted Tail, who had recently been made chief of all the Sioux over Red Cloud, wanted no rivals either. Although his agency was forty miles to the east, he, too, began to feel threatened by Crazy Horse's growing influence. ''The talk that he was to be made chief over all was causing intense jealousy,'' an onlooker commented.

Spotted Tail's protests and Red Cloud's whispering campaign were effective. Although the soldiers admired Crazy Horse, the presence of the great Oglala and his warriors at the agency made them nervous and they called off both the buffalo hunt and the feast. Crazy Horse was disappointed but not surprised. More white promises broken.

Still Red Cloud wasn't satisfied. The whites have no intention of ever giving you your own agency, he told Crazy Horse. More than that, when you come back from Washington, they're going to put you in chains and ship you to jail on an island off the coast of Florida.

Chains and jail! The worst horror of all!

Red Cloud wasn't finished. He next arranged for Nellie Larrabee, the daughter of a white trader and a Sioux mother, to come live in Crazy Horse's lodge as his second wife. Many men had more than one wife and the arrangement was acceptable to Black Shawl. Although her health was better, she still hadn't much strength and Nellie took over her heaviest chores. Nellie, however, also began to work on Crazy Horse. The trip to Washington was a trap set by the soldiers, she insisted.

Once again, Crazy Horse changed his mind. "I am not going there," he told White Hat Clark. "Still deep in my heart I hold that place on Beaver Creek where I want my agency. You have my horses and my guns. I have only my tent and my will. You got me to come here and you can keep me here by force if you choose, but you cannot make me go anywhere that I refuse to go."

In the end, the furor came to nothing. Faced with a military crisis, the Army postponed the trip to Washington. A band of Nez Percés under Chief Joseph, who had rebelled against being moved from their Oregon homeland, were headed for the Powder River country. With the defeat of the last Sioux holdouts under Chief Lame Deer by Bear Coat Miles on May 7, there were no Sioux left in the Powder River country. They were all on agencies except for Sitting Bull and his Hunkpapas who had fled to Canada.

The Nez Percé situation was so serious that White Hat was ordered to recruit Oglala warriors as scouts. White Hat met in council with several Sioux leaders, including Crazy Horse and Touch-the-Clouds. When asked to have his men serve as scouts, Crazy Horse responded, "We are tired of war; we came in for peace, but now that the Great Father asks our help, we will go north and fight until there is not a Nez Percé left!"

Whether intentionally or not, the fort interpreter translated Crazy Horse's reply as: "We will go north and fight until not a white man is left!" Instantly the council was in an uproar. White Hat, sure that Crazy Horse meant to go on the warpath, was furious. And when Crazy Horse said that he wanted to take along the women and children and do a little hunting on the side, White Hat became even angrier. At that point, Crazy Horse, tired of the squabbling, walked out of the council, while Touch-the-Clouds rode back to the Spotted Tail Agency where he lived.

The error in translation was straightened out a day or two later, but by then it was too late. Panicked, Clark had already gotten in touch with senior Army officials, who, in turn, had ordered Three Stars Crook to return to Camp Robinson and take over. As soon as Three Stars arrived on September 2, 1877, he directed all the Sioux to move across nearby White Clay Creek for a council.

Although two officers were sent to Crazy Horse's lodge with the order, Crazy Horse was suspicious of their gifts of cigars and a knife and he told them that he wouldn't go. "He thought the gift of a knife meant trouble coming," He Dog said. "He thought they shook hands with him as if they did not mean him any good. He was afraid there would be trouble at that council."

He Dog, on the other hand, was concerned for the safety of the women and children. "Does this mean that you will be my enemy if I move across the creek?'' he asked Crazy Horse.

Crazy Horse laughed. "I am no white man!'' he said. "They are the only people that make rules for other people, that say, 'If you stay on one side of this line it is peace; but if you go on the other side, I will kill you all.' I don't hold with deadlines. There is plenty of room; camp where you please."

As it turned out, the council was never held anyway. On his way to meet with the Sioux, Three Stars was stopped by Woman's Dress, the same *winkte* who had told Crazy Horse that Black Buffalo Woman had married No Water. Now Woman's Dress warned Three Stars that Crazy Horse planned to kill him and his officers at the council. Three Stars immediately canceled the council and called together all the friendly Sioux head men. Although some suggested that he have Crazy Horse killed, Three Stars refused to commit outright murder. Instead he ordered Crazy Horse's arrest. Leaving the whole thorny problem in White Hat Clark's hands, Three Stars conveniently left that night for the Powder River country.

Luckily, Red Feather heard about the arrest-order and warned Crazy Horse. Crazy Horse knew that he had done nothing, threatened no one. He hadn't even tried to leave the agency. And now he was to be arrested. White justice again! Quickly he rounded up ponies for Black Shawl and himself and together they started out for the Spotted Tail Agency forty miles away. It was their last chance to find peace.

CHAPTER 29

Red Feather had spoken true. The next morning, September 4, 1877, White Hat Clark, his troops, Red Cloud and a number of Sioux volunteers, including three of Crazy Horse's own warriors, Little Big Man, Big Road and Jumping Shield, headed out to arrest Crazy Horse. But they found his camp deserted. Red Feather reported that White Hat "went back to the fort and called together all the scouts. White Hat offered $100 and a sorrel horse to any Indian who would kill Crazy Horse."

No Water, Black Buffalo Woman's husband, who had shot Crazy Horse years ago in a jealous rage, was one of the first to ride out in pursuit. He set such a hard pace in his zeal to catch Crazy Horse that two ponies died under him.

Despite their pursuers, Crazy Horse and Black Shawl reached the Spotted Tail Agency safely. There they were greeted by Touch-the-Clouds and Lieutenant Jesse Lee, the military Indian Agent in charge of the agency, who believed that the whole problem was simply the result of a misunderstanding. Spotted Tail was there, too, but he no more wanted a rival for his position than Red Cloud did.

"We never have trouble here! The sky is clear; the air still and free from dust," he told Crazy Horse. "I am chief here! . . . Every Indian who comes here must obey me! You say you want to come to this Agency to live peaceably. If you stay here, you must listen to me! That is all!"

Crazy Horse explained to Spotted Tail and Agent Lee that he only wanted to be left alone, that he had never planned to go on the warpath or kill Three Stars. All those bad things said about him were lies. Following much talk, it was decided that he and Black Shawl could move to the Spotted Tail Agency but only after Crazy Horse had returned to the Red Cloud Agency and straightened out the misunderstanding. Although Crazy Horse sensed that he was in for more lies . . . and danger, Lee convinced him that his people might be in trouble if he didn't clear up the matter. As always, Crazy Horse put his people first and he agreed to return.

The next morning, Crazy Horse headed back to Camp Robinson, accompanied by Lee, Touch-the-Clouds and a number of Sioux warriors. When they arrived late in the afternoon, Camp Robinson's parade ground was thronged with thousands of Sioux who had heard of the trouble and awaited Crazy Horse's return. He Dog was there, too, wearing his war bonnet. "I rode up on the left side of Crazy Horse and shook hands with him. I saw that he did not look right. I said, 'Look out—watch your step—you are going into a dangerous place.' "

Little Big Man, another warrior who had fought alongside of Crazy Horse in almost every battle, rode on Crazy Horse's right side. Although Crazy Horse knew that He Dog was

163

trustworthy, Little Big Man now wore an agency police uniform and worked for the white soldiers.

Crazy Horse dismounted in front of the adjutant's office, a guard on either side of him. Another soldier marched up and down outside the door, a bayoneted gun on his shoulder. It was late, the adjutant said, and he couldn't see Crazy Horse now. He would see him in the morning. (The next morning the Army planned to send Crazy Horse to prison off the coast of Florida just as Red Cloud had warned.)

With Little Big Man gripping his arm, Crazy Horse walked toward the dark building next to the adjutant's office where he was to spend the night. But as he stepped inside, a terrible stench assailed him and in the dim light from a tiny air hole in the ceiling, he saw several men in chains. This was the guardhouse! He was to be locked up! Instinctively, Crazy Horse jerked his arm away from Little Big Man and pulled out a knife that he had hidden in his leggings. As he ran for the door, he lashed out wildly at the officer of the day who deflected the blow with his sword.

And then Crazy Horse and the men around him were outside in a scuffling of shouts and confusion. Jennie Fast Thunder, who was one of the stunned onlookers, remembered the moment. "He rushed out and I heard him using the brave word—the word a warrior uses when he wishes to keep up his courage—'H'g un.' "

Others were yelling, too. "Kill him! Kill him!" bellowed the officer of the day as nearby guards sprang forward with their bayonets at the ready. Still striking out with his knife, Crazy Horse slashed Little Big Man across the forearm. Despite his wound, Little Big Man seized Crazy Horse's arms at the elbows and pinned them behind his back. One of his own people prevented him from defending himself. It was just as

164

his vision had foreshadowed more than twenty years before.

Remembering how Little Big Man had restrained him on the day that No Water had shot him, Crazy Horse shouted, "You have done this once before." With a desperate lunge, he broke free at the instant a soldier jabbed a bayonet into his back. The thrust from another bayonet pierced his kidney. Crazy Horse staggered and fell.

"They stabbed me," he cried. Little Big Man and a number of the guards grabbed for Crazy Horse but he stopped them. "Let me go, my friends. You have got me hurt bad enough."

He Dog hurried to his friend's side. "There were soldiers standing all around him," He Dog recalled. "The bayonet was laying on the ground beside him and also the knife he had used, and they were red. I tore in two the large red agency blanket which I was wearing and used half of it to cover him. He was gasping hard for breath. 'See where I am hurt,' he gasped. 'I can feel the blood flowing.'"

Touch-the-Clouds was there, too. With his seven-foot height towering over everyone, he stopped the guards from dragging the wounded Crazy Horse into the jail. "He was a great chief and he cannot be put in prison," Touch-the-Clouds told them. Bending over, he picked up the slender Crazy Horse and carried him into the adjutant's office. It was only after Dr. McGillicuddy arrived with morphine that Crazy Horse's pain was eased.

Worm was sent for, too. "Son, I am here," he repeated over and over.

Crazy Horse, who had asked to be laid on the floor rather than on a cot, opened his eyes. "A-h-h-h, my father, I am bad hurt. Tell the people it is no use to depend on me any more now. I am going to die." An hour or so later, shortly before

165

midnight on September 5, 1877, just four months after his surrender, Crazy Horse died.

Touch-the-Clouds went outside to tell the waiting, silent people. These were the warriors who had followed Crazy Horse into battle, the women and helpless ones to whom he had given his ponies and meat from the hunt, the children whom he had taught the ways of the Oglalas. "It is good," Touch-the-Clouds told them. "He has looked for death, and it has come."

"Before he was buried a war-eagle came to walk about on the coffin every night. It did nothing, only just walked about."

Red Feather

"His parents placed his body on a *travois* and took it away, burying it secretly. Whenever anyone asked his wife about the grave of her husband she always replied, 'I shall never tell anyone where he is; it was your jealousy that killed him.' His parents never told anyone where they put the body of their son and no living Sioux knows where it is."

Jennie Fast Thunder

"He never wanted anything but to save his people . . . It does not matter where his body lies, for it is grass; but where his spirit is, it will be good to be."

Black Elk

166

EPILOGUE

There is much about the life of *Tashunka Witko,* or Crazy Horse, that remains a mystery. (*Tashunka* means Horse, while *Witko* means Strange, Mystical or Awe-inspiring.) Neither the year of Crazy Horse's birth nor where his body is buried is known for sure. Little has come down to us about his childhood. He refused ever to be photographed. Only accounts and interviews with those who knew him have survived and these accounts are sometimes contradictory. Even details of his most famous battle, the Battle of the Little Bighorn, are still hotly debated.

One fact is certain, though. Great a warrior as Crazy Horse may have been, he was, in the end, much more. He was a man whose deepest love and concern was for his people and their well-being. And for that he will always be remembered.

BIBLIOGRAPHY

Ambrose, Stephen E. *Crazy Horse and Custer.* Garden City, New York: Doubleday and Company, Inc., 1975.

Anderson, Harry H. "Indian Peace-Talkers and the Conclusion of the Sioux War of 1876," *Nebraska History,* Lincoln: Nebraska State Historical Society, December 1963, Vol. 44, No. 4, p. 233–254.

"The Battle of Blue Water, September 3, 1855." *Ash Hollow, A State Historical Park.* Nebraska Game and Parks Commission, p. 1–45.

Blish, Helen H. *A Pictographic History of the Oglala Sioux.* Lincoln, Nebraska: University of Nebraska Press, 1967.

Bourke, John G. *On the Border with Crook.* Lincoln, Nebraska: University of Nebraska Press, 1971.

Brininstool, E. A. *Crazy Horse, the Invincible Oglala Sioux.* Los Angeles, California: Wetzel Publishing Co. Inc., 1949.

———. "How Crazy Horse Died." *Nebraska History Magazine.* Lincoln, Nebraska: Nebraska State Historical Society, January–March 1929, Vol. XII, No. 1, p. 1–78.

Brown, Dee. *The Fetterman Massacre.* Lincoln, Nebraska: University of Nebraska Press, 1971.

Brown, Vinson. *Crazy Horse, Hoka Hey! (It is a good time to die!).* Happy Camp, California: Naturegraph Publishers, Inc., 1987.

Clark, Robert A. *The Killing of Crazy Horse.* Glendale, California: The Arthur H. Clark Company, 1976.

Eastman, Charles A. *Indian Heroes and Great Chieftains.* Boston: Little, Brown and Co., 1918.

Finerty, John F. *War-Path and Bivouac: The Big Horn and Yellowstone Expedition.* Norman, Oklahoma: University of Oklahoma Press, 1961.

Garnett, William. "Report of William Garnett, Interpreter to General H. L. Scott and Major James McLaughlin." *Westerner.* November 1858.

Gilbert, James N. "The Death of Crazy Horse." *Journal of the West.* January 1993, Vol. XXXII, No. 1.

Graham, Colonel W. A. *The Custer Myth.* New York: Bonanza Books, 1953.

Gray, John S. "The Pack Train on George A. Custer's Last Campaign." *Nebraska History.* Spring 1976, Vol. 57, No. 1, p. 53–68.

Grinnell, George Bird. *The Fighting Cheyennes.* Norman, Oklahoma: University of Oklahoma Press, 1955.

————. *When Buffalo Ran.* New Haven, Connecticut: Yale University Press, 1920.

Hardoff, Richard G. *The Oglala Lakota Crazy Horse.* Mattituck, New York: J.M. Carroll & Company, 1985.

Hassrick, Royal B. *The Sioux, Life and Customs of a Warrior Society.* Norman, Oklahoma: University of Oklahoma Press, 1964.

Hinman, Eleanor H. "Oglala Sources on the Life of Crazy Horse." *Nebraska History.* Lincoln, Nebraska: Nebraska State Historical Society. Spring 1976, Vol. 57, No. 1, p. 1–51.

Hook, Jason. *Crazy Horse, Sacred Warrior of the Sioux.* New York: Firebird Books Ltd., 1989.

Hyde, George. *Red Cloud's Folk. A History of the Oglala Sioux Indians.* Norman, Oklahoma: University of Oklahoma Press, 1937.

————. *Spotted Tail's Folk. A History of the Brulé Sioux.* Norman, Oklahoma: University of Oklahoma Press, 1961.

Kadlecek, Edward and Mabell. *To Kill an Eagle, Indian Views on the Last Days of Crazy Horse.* Boulder, Colorado: Johnson Publishing Co., 1981.

Keenan, Jerry. *The Wagon Box Fight.* Sheridan, Wyoming: The Fort Phil Kearny/Bozeman Trail Association, 1990.

King, James T. "Needed: A Re-Evaluation of General George Crook," *Nebraska History,* Lincoln: Nebraska State Historical Society, September 1964, Vol. 45, No. 3, p. 226–235.

Knight, Oliver. "War or Peace: The Anxious Wait for Crazy Horse," *Nebraska,* Lincoln: Nebraska State Historical Society, Winter 1973, Vol. 54, No. 4, p. 521–544.

Laubin, Reginald and Gladys. *The Indian Tipi, Its History, Construction, and Use.* New York: Ballantine Books, 1971.

Lavender, David. *Fort Laramie and the Changing Frontier.* Washington, D.C.: Division of Publications, National Park Service, 1983.

McCann, Lloyd E. "The Grattan Massacre." *Nebraska History*. Lincoln, Nebraska: Nebraska State Historical Society, March 1956, Vol. XXXVII, No. 1.

Mattison, Ray H., Ed. "The Harney Expedition Against the Sioux: The Journal of Captain John B. S. Todd," *Nebraska History,* Lincoln: Nebraska State Historical Society, June 1962, Vol. 43, No. 2, p. 89–130.

Mears, David Y. "Campaigning Against Crazy Horse." *Nebraska State Historical Society,* Series II. Lincoln, Nebraska: Jacob North & Co., Printers, 1907, Vol. 15, p. 68 ff.

Moeller, Bill and Jan. *Crazy Horse, His Life, His Lands, A Photographic Biography.* Wilsonville, Oregon: Beautiful America Publishing Co., 1987.

Nadeau, Remi. *Fort Laramie and the Sioux Indians.* Englewood Cliffs, New Jersey: Prentice-Hall, Inc., 1967.

Neihardt, John G. *Black Elk Speaks.* Lincoln, Nebraska: University of Nebraska Press, 1979.

Olson, James C. *Red Cloud and the Sioux Problem.* Lincoln, Nebraska: University of Nebraska Press, 1965.

Parkman, Francis. *The Oregon Trail.* New York: New American Library, Inc., 1950.

Ricker, Judge E. S. "Part of his Project for a History of the Plains Indians." From the Historical Library of Judge E. S. Ricker. Received by the Nebraska State Historical Society, November 2, 1926.

Rickey, Don. "The Battle of Wolf Mountain." *Montana, the Magazine of Western History.* Helena, Montana: The Historical Society of Montana, Spring 1963, Vol. XIII, No. 2, p. 44–54.

Robinson, Doane. *A History of the Dakota or Sioux Indians.* Aberdeen, South Dakota: News Printing Co., 1904.

Sandoz, Mari. *The Buffalo Hunters.* New York: Hastings House, Publishers, 1954.

————. *Crazy Horse, The Strange Man of the Oglalas.* Lincoln, Nebraska: University of Nebraska Press, 1992.

————. *Hostiles and Friendlies.* Lincoln, Nebraska: University of Nebraska Press, 1959.

————. *These Were the Sioux.* New York: Hastings House Publishers, 1961.

Standing Bear, Luther. *Land of the Spotted Eagle.* Lincoln, Nebraska: University of Nebraska Press, 1978.

————. *My Indian Boyhood.* Lincoln, Nebraska: University of Nebraska Press, 1988.

————. *My People the Sioux.* Boston, Massachusetts: Houghton Mifflin Co., Inc., 1928.

Stands in Timber, John. "Last Ghastly Moments at the Little Bighorn." *American Heritage.* New York: American Heritage Publishing Co., April 1966, Vol. XVII, No. 3, p. 4 ff.

Stewart, Edgar I. *Custer's Luck*. Norman, Oklahoma: University of Oklahoma Press, 1955.

Tibbles, T. H. "Death of Logan Fontanelle." *Story by Iron Eye*. Lincoln, Nebraska: Nebraska State Historical Society, Second Series, 1902, Vol. V., p. 161 ff.

Utley, Robert M. *Custer Battlefield, A History and Guide to The Battle of the Little Bighorn*. Washington, D.C.: Division of Publications, National Park Service, 1988.

————. *Frontier Regulars*. New York: Macmillan Publishing Co., Inc., 1973.

————. *The Lance and the Shield: The Life and Times of Sitting Bull*. New York: Henry Holt and Company, 1993.

Vestal, Stanley. "The Man Who Killed Custer," *American Heritage*. New York: American Heritage Publishing Co., February 1957, Vol. VIII, No. 2, p. 14 ff.

———— *Sitting Bull, Champion of the Sioux*. Norman, Oklahoma: University of Oklahoma Press, 1957.

———— *Warpath and Council Fire*. New York: Random House, 1948.

172

INDEX

174

176